LES

SAM EAVIS

Lessons in Art first published in 2011 by
Chimera Books Ltd
PO Box 152
Waterlooville
Hants
PO8 9FS
United Kingdom

Printed and bound in the UK by
Cox & Wyman, Reading.

ISBN 978-1-907976-07-0

This novel is fiction – in real life practice safe sex

This book is sold subject to the condition that it shall not, by way of trade or otherwise, be lent, resold, hired out or otherwise circulated without the publisher's prior written consent in any form of binding or cover other than that in which it is published, and without a similar condition being imposed on the subsequent purchaser.

The characters and situations in this book are entirely imaginary and bear no relation to any real person or actual happening.

Copyright © Sam Eavis

The right of Sam Eavis to be identified as author of this book has been asserted in accordance with section 77 and 78 of the Copyrights Designs and Patents Act 1988.

LESSONS IN ART

Sam Eavis

Chimera *(kī-mîr′ə, kĭ-)* a creation of the imagination, a wild fantasy

Rather ominously James took her wrists and fastened them into the cuffs low down on the bench, and then he strapped her ankles and thighs with leather bands also fitted to it. He adjusted the buckles so her legs were held tightly together, then finally a belt which hung from one side of the bench top was drawn tightly over her waist and fastened into its buckle on the opposite side.

Nicola was so tightly squeezed into the bench that she could hardly move an inch...

Chapter 1

Sir James Hammond brought his eyes back from the tall windows of his study and the winter's first snow falling gently outside. He reclined further in the leather chair and surveyed the girl standing in front of his large mahogany desk with renewed interest. A typical twenty-something, whose main interests were probably drinking and clubbing with her friends; this had been his view of her until now. Certainly, it had seemed that Nicola's job as his secretary, the latest in a number of short periods of similar employment, was not the highest priority in her life. He had only taken her on at all as a favour to an old friend, who had become her guardian after the death of her parents.

This Monday morning it appeared that her job meant more to her than she had previously cared to show. Probably the expensive run-up to Christmas had brought it home to her. She had apologised profusely for the costly mistake and, as far as he could tell, she was genuinely sorry about it.

'That's all very well, Nicola, but this isn't the first time.' In fact she had forgotten to pass on instructions to his stockbroker on two previous occasions in the last three months. She stood with her hands by her side looking down at the desk before her, a picture of despondency.

'I hadn't realised that a short delay could cost so much. You were very kind about the others.' Her voice broke a little.

The last thing he wanted was for her to start crying. He tried to put some softness in his voice as he stated his grievance. 'It's true the others were less of a problem but I still lost money. This time the shares rose so quickly after start of trading that it cost me nearly twenty thousand pounds more to buy them.'

'But why do you have to sack me? You've said I'm good at my job sometimes. And I can't tell you how much I like working for you.' The catch in her voice was still there.

James had heard this sort of flattery before from young people who didn't want to lose comfortable and well-paid jobs, but didn't want to put much effort into them either.

'I need a secretary I can rely on to carry out my orders promptly,' he said, gently.

It seemed a reasonable requirement to him but she didn't seem inclined to accept it. He wondered what more he could say to make her leave without any tears. He had to admit she looked very pretty, standing there so forlornly, her bob-cut blonde hair hanging slightly forward round her face. James had always found her distractingly lovely, but work had to come first.

Suddenly she looked up at him and asked, 'Can't you punish me in some other way?'

He was a little surprised at her choice of word. It seemed that her hazel eyes were imploring him to understand an unspoken proposal. He needed to be clear what she meant.

'How? I could hardly deduct it from your salary.'

'I didn't mean that,' she said. 'I was working late that night last week when you...' she paused, clearly uncertain how to phrase what she had seen. Finally she said, 'I heard you discussing the Amex bill with your fiancée.'

Now he understood her. He had given Rebecca a new Centurion card on his account with firm instructions to go easy. Instead she had melted her new plastic in forty-eight hours. He had let her keep the card but at a price to be paid lying across an armchair with her backside in the air. It was not an infrequent occurrence for Rebecca, who tended to be rather wilful and headstrong, not traits James wished to encourage in his wife-to-be. And he had wanted to give her a salutary reminder before she went off to Italy skiing with her girlfriends this week.

Before lowering her eyes again Nicola glanced meaningfully towards a cabinet in the corner of the study. The top of the cabinet held drinks and a selection of glasses. He knew, though, that she was looking towards the cupboard beneath.

He made up his mind to fall in with her wishes, but it would be on his terms. He regarded her in silence for a minute or so while he decided exactly what those terms would be. He moved his eyes up her body. Black leather high heels and black stockings led to a black miniskirt, which hugged her legs and the contours of her hips. A close-fitting short-sleeved white blouse came to just below the waistband of her skirt. Beneath the thin cotton he could make out a white bra. Apart from a gold watch, her only jewellery was a simple gold band around her neck. James thought that she always dressed far too sexily for this job. She's a flirtatious minx, too, he thought. She often took the opportunity to lean over his desk, giving him a view of her cleavage or her tight-skirted bottom according to her whim.

'Take your blouse off.' He didn't really know what made him say it, except that he'd always found it difficult to resist submissive beauty. Perhaps, too, he wanted to repay those flashes of bare flesh. He would see how flirtatious she felt now, as he took advantage of her penitence.

He half expected her to cry out in astonished protest. But instead Nicola looked up and smiled at him, no doubt taking this to mean her job was safe. She even said, 'Thank you,' quickly unbuttoning the blouse before he had time to change his mind.

She stood more confidently before him, her stomach toned and waist slender. As she breathed he could see her breasts move gently, cupped by the white bra. White now looked incongruous against the black clothes below. Her new coolness goaded him further. 'Remove your bra as well.'

He thought she would baulk at this but she didn't. She simply removed it and put it with her blouse over the guest chair by her side. Her mood had brightened and she was not in the least embarrassed by standing half naked before him. Admittedly, with her body she had nothing to be embarrassed about. She stood straight, legs together and arms by her sides as if she was a young cadet told to report to the colonel. Instead of looking at the floor as before she now kept her eyes on the desktop. Her nipples were erect and James realised she was at least a little aroused by her situation. He was guiltily aware too that he hadn't needed her topless to deal out a beating. He was getting in very deeply for an engaged man, but it was too late to back out now.

'I think you know what is in the cabinet. Bring out both items and put them on the desk.'

Nicola approached the cabinet. Quite deliberately she stopped a little before it and bent slowly forward, legs straight and firmly together. She's a tease, he thought, and soon he would make her pay for it, but for the moment he simply admired her shapely legs, the pale skin now showing between the tops of her stockings and the lovely peach shape of the buttock-stretched skirt.

From the lower cupboard Nicola took out a thirty-inch school cane and a broad leather strap, slowly straightened up and brought them to the desk.

'Caning is very painful and is not something everyone can bear. I need to know if you have ever been caned before.'

'My guardian caned me when I deserved it.'

'I see.' He had always suspected his amiable old friend Edward of being a martinet in his own home. 'When were you last caned?'

'When I was twenty. He said it would be my future partner's job after I "came of age", as he put it.'

Nicola was obviously a much more complex girl than he had imagined. He couldn't believe that many young adults would stand for such treatment from their parents, let alone guardians. James overcame his surprise. He was interested to see more of the bottom which had grown accustomed to firm handling in the past.

'Well I see that you know the sort of thing to expect. Even so, it may be best for you to hear my terms before you agree.'

She nodded, her eyes bright with nervous expectation.

'Now take off your skirt.'

She slowly removed it, revealing stay-up stockings and the black triangle of her thong. It must have been obvious to her that he liked what he saw, and he was about to ask her to turn round when she did so anyway, standing with her back to him to show off what he really wanted to see most.

'Bend over and touch your toes. Stay like that until I tell you to rise.'

He was very aroused as he watched her slowly bend forward, her buttocks rounding either side of the thin line of the thong. She gripped her ankles to hold herself in position - not quite what he had asked for but he would let it pass.

'You may keep your job now and for as long as you wish to accept corporal punishment for your mistakes. If at any time you change your mind you must leave, but I will give you a satisfactory reference.'

'Thank you, sir.'

'Now, Nicola, this was a serious mistake which requires a severe punishment; perhaps more severe than you've had before. You will receive six strokes of the strap on your bottom, followed by six strokes of the cane. I will decide the appropriate degree of clothing.' He paused. 'If any,' he added.

'Yes, sir,' she said, still bent over.

'I've not quite finished. You will receive the same treatment, repeated on Wednesday and Friday this week, before you leave work.' He heard her gasp a little, but she remained in place.

'In total that is thirty-six strokes, which works out at over five hundred pounds per stroke. You can see that your education is rather an expensive exercise on my part. Let's hope you learn from it. Tuesday and Thursday will be recovery days. I think you will be grateful for them.'

She said nothing and he was prompted to push her further.

'You must remain bent over to receive the strokes until I tell you to rise. You may cry out but you must not swear. Failure to follow these or any other rules I set will mean extra strokes. In addition, I may choose to give you a hand spanking whenever I deem it to be suitable.

'You may ask me to stop at any time before the punishment is over, in which case you will leave my employment with the reference I promised. Stand up and face me.'

Her colour had heightened during this little speech and her breathing was definitely pronounced. James' mind was beginning to wander a little. Nicola was so compliant to his wishes that he wondered how the punishment would develop. He knew well enough that it would lead to complications with Rebecca if she found out. He thought he saw a twinkle in Nicola's eyes. She knows it too, he thought. Well, his ruminations had given her long enough to think about her decision.

'Are those terms acceptable to you?' he asked. Life would be a lot easier if she just said no. But her face, flushed with excitement, and her nipples, as prominent and firm as before, had given him her answer already.

'Yes sir, they are.'

He hesitated before casting the die. 'Very well. We shall begin at six o'clock this evening. Before you go back to your office put the cane and strap away.'

James watched her dress and leave. Suddenly he felt a little uneasy as to what the future may hold.

Just before six o'clock there was a light knock on the door and Nicola entered.

No extra strokes for lateness then, thought James. As she walked in he could faintly smell her pleasant perfume even from his desk. She had clearly freshened herself up. She seemed expectant but not otherwise unnerved by the imminent ordeal. He wondered whether she truly could endure the beating so calmly. They would soon see.

James was a man who liked to get down to business with as little delay as possible. He told Nicola to remove her blouse and bra as she had done earlier, but this time to leave her skirt on. He ordered her to fetch the cane and strap and put them on the desk before her. She did as he said and stood before his desk waiting, naked from the waist up, as cool as if she were about to take dictation.

'Are you going to spank me first?' she asked quietly.

Suddenly he felt an urge to shatter her calm and make her suffer for her mistake - after all, she had cost him a small fortune by her standards.

'Not today. We'll get straight to the more severe part of the punishment.'

She heard the harsh note in his voice and looked at him a little fearfully. She'll soon realise this is not a game, he thought.

'Hands on your head and bend over!' he barked.

From the front of the desk she lent forward towards him, hands on head, stopping when her nipples touched the inlaid leather of the desktop. He moved round behind her.

'When we come to the caning you may put your forearms on the desk. For the duration of the strapping your hands will stay on your head. If you move them you will receive an extra stroke.'

He admired her position from the rear and side: feet together in their glossy black heels, perfectly straight legs and dipped back presenting her bottom to await the strap. Her upper body was almost totally still, with her hanging breasts just resting on the desktop.

James approached her and laid a hand on each buttock, apparently smoothing the already tight material across her bottom. Nicola kept perfectly still. After a few moments he took up the strap and positioned himself slightly behind her to her left. He paused for a good thirty seconds to let her feel the anticipation of the first stroke. Then he swung the eighteen-inch shaft of leather fiercely across her right buttock.

Nicola's soft cry was almost drowned by the loud report of the leather on her behind. It had been a hard stroke for the first but she hardly moved. He swung again, another full stroke, this time landing equally across both buttocks. Again she gasped gently. After counting slowly to twenty he delivered another similar stroke. The thwack of the leather resounded in the still, oak-panelled study, but Nicola made little sound and maintained her posture well.

James put down the strap and stood behind her. He carefully rolled the skirt up over her bottom to reveal beautiful cheeks, now reddened in several places. After settling her skirt so it would not slip down, he moved his hands again over her bottom, gently squeezing and caressing. He could hear her breathing a little more deeply now.

He picked up the strap again and, taking up the same position behind her, began the remainder of her strapping. Three fierce strokes thwacked across her bottom, twenty seconds apart. This time her cheeks were unprotected, with the thong offering no cover at all. He could see the flesh flatten as the strap hit its target. And he could see the cheeks begin to glow a deeper red in places where the strap hit directly, spreading pink over the remainder of her bottom. As the last hard stroke landed Nicola jumped slightly and let out a louder cry of pain. Even so, she was taking it very well.

As James lay down the strap he leaned forward towards Nicola's ear.

'Is this firm enough discipline for you, young lady?' he said quietly.

'Yes, sir,' she replied calmly.

'Well I'm sorry to say it's about to get much firmer. I wonder if you'll feel as sure of yourself this time on Friday evening.'

Nicola gave a rueful little laugh, and he knew she knew that the week could be an unnerving ordeal.

'Stay bending over the desk, but you may lower your hands now.' He heard her sigh of relief as she rested her stiff arms on the desktop. For a moment she started to move her hands back to feel her bottom, but he quickly forbade it.

'You may not touch yourself, unless you want extra strokes of the cane.'

She groaned a little and braced herself. James retreated to one of the large leather armchairs which stood, together with a Chesterfield sofa, by the fireplace. For five minutes he watched the slight wriggles of her body as she tried to make her position more comfortable. Neither said a word but the atmosphere was sharp with anticipation.

Then he rose and went over to her, unzipped her skirt and let it drop to the floor. She neatly stepped out of it without getting up and he kicked it to one side. Gently he lowered her thong over her bottom and midway down her thighs.

James picked up the cane from the desk and held it just above her bottom. Nicola's position had slackened a little.

'Straighten your back and push out your bottom,' he said, and as she did so the soft skin of her buttocks touched the cane as he held it in position. He let it rest there a moment.

'It seems I'm doing all the work here. Now I'd like you to count each stroke.'

He swished the cane through the air a few times and watched her. Not a flicker. He took the accustomed stance behind her and laid the cane across her bare buttocks, gently moving it up and down over the skin. Still no reaction from her. He paused, then raised the cane and brought it sharply down across both cheeks.

It was not a very hard stroke but it did elicit a response. She cried out quite sharply and for a moment was about to move her hands to her bottom, but held back just in time. She's remembered how much it stings, he thought, watching a red line appear where the stroke had landed.

'Well?' he said.

'Sorry. One, sir.'

He rested the cane on her bottom again and waited for a moment. He raised it and swept down a second stroke of similar power. She gave a soft grunt but no more as a second red line appeared parallel to the first.

'Two, sir,' she counted.

He continued with another stroke in a similar

vein, then stopped. He looked down at the three red lines across her bottom. Nicola had controlled herself well, barely crying out or moving as the cane beat her. He admired her courage, but it made him want to be crueller still.

'No penalty strokes yet, young lady. I wonder if you'll manage to get through today without any.' He paused. 'By the way, the last three strokes will be rather harder than the previous three.' Nicola sighed faintly and he saw her grip her hands tightly together on the desktop. Then she lowered her forehead to rest on them, her shiny blonde hair falling over her wrists. She was bracing herself for worse to come.

James whipped in the fourth blow across the middle of her behind. Nicola yelped loudly, struggling to hold her posture. He could sense her screwing up her face with the pain for some seconds before she was able to speak the number of the stroke. Her panties had fallen down her legs to the floor and she stepped from them to stop her heels catching. He picked them up with the tip of the cane and deposited them on the chair.

For the fifth stroke he rested the cane just below her buttocks. Knowing what was to come she groaned slightly. He paused, aiming carefully to make sure he hit the narrow target above her stocking tops and did not fall lower to the backs of her thighs; he wanted no welts visible below her short skirts.

The cane cracked harshly across the top of each leg. Immediately a raised red line began to appear. Nicola's body shook as she cried out in pain. She lifted her right foot, holding the leg bent for some time as she fought to keep herself down. Now her breathing came heavy and fast. James was grimly satisfied.

At last I'm getting to her, he thought.

Eventually she lowered her foot again and gasped, 'Five, sir.'

He waited a full minute to let her settle before putting the cane in place across her bottom for the final stroke. Then suddenly he moved it away and quickly swished it in the air without hitting her, to see her reaction. Her buttocks clenched and she moved forward in anticipation of the blow, and relaxed back into place when it didn't come. At that moment he raised his arm back behind his head and quickly lashed the cane across her cheeks, so hard it bent almost fully around her right side.

This was too much. Nicola jerked upright and let out a piercing yowl. Her hands flew to her buttocks.

'Agh... fucking hell!' she screamed.

He waited while she held her welted buttocks in her hands, stepping from foot to foot and still yelping as the agonising stinging persisted. He wondered if she would back out now and leave his employ. He was no longer sure another two sessions would be possible. But she had stayed facing the desk and appeared to have calmed down, although still breathing deeply. She eventually let her hands fall to her sides.

'Six, sir,' she said quietly.

Although she'd had enough he knew she

expected him to be as strict as he had promised. He therefore said, 'I'm afraid you broke the rules on the last stroke, Nicola.' She waited in silence.

'I'll deliver just two extra strokes, one for swearing and one for standing up before I allowed you to. Resume your position.'

She obeyed, again resting her head on tightly clasped hands. Even now she bent over well, legs together and perfectly straight, offering her red buttocks for the further chastisement.

'Ready? Let's try to make these the last for today.'

Nevertheless he made them hard strokes, whipping across welts from earlier strokes and making her whole body shudder with pain. She kept steady and muffled her yelps into the desktop, but each time she had to wait to recover before counting the stroke.

At the end he surveyed his work for a minute or two before allowing her to rise. Faint blue bruises were appearing on some of the cane marks. When he told her to stand she stretched in relief from the stiffness of holding her position for so long.

Seated again at his desk, to hide his erection, he watched while she gingerly dressed herself. Then she stood before him, apparently waiting for permission to leave. James' own emotions were becoming complex. He wondered what, apart from the after-effects of her painful session, she was feeling.

'Now you know what it's like do you wish to continue with our arrangement?'

There was a pause and he worried this might be

the last time he saw her. He thought she sensed his concern and tried to muster a weak smile.

'Yes. I deserve it, don't I?'

As she was about to leave he realised there was something he had not thought of until now.

'What will your boyfriend say when he sees the marks on your bottom?'

'I've split up with him,' she said simply, and left the room.

Chapter 2

Any guilty unease James felt at the conclusion of the morning's interview with Nicola would have been replaced by rage had he been able to see Rebecca at that moment. She was reclining on the bed in a tiny attic flat in Milan, divested of all items of clothing, skiing or otherwise, in the classic pose of Velázquez's famous Venus. A young artist stood at his easel painting her. He worked quickly with intense concentration, making the most of the thin sunlight.

Lying with her back to him Rebecca could admire his reflection in a mirror, of the type held by Cupid in the Rokeby masterpiece. With his dark good looks and suppressed virility Carlo was undoubtedly more overtly attractive than James. But Rebecca had no taste for long term relationships with penniless young artists - even those as talented as Carlo. James adored her and, most conveniently, he was wealthier than even a highly successful artist was ever likely to be.

The young painter was proving himself to be a perfectionist. Although dispensing with Cupid, he had insisted on the remaining scene being as close to Velázquez's original as possible: white and grey silk sheets on the bed; a rich red curtain in the background. Rebecca's deep chestnut hair was a close enough match, but Carlo had brought in an expensive stylist who had expertly replicated Venus's untidy bun.

After a period of silence Carlo paused and looked across at her. 'You have seen the Venus in your National Gallery?'

'Of course,' she replied, a little irritably. It should have been obvious to him that Rebecca, an executive in a firm of art galleries, would be familiar with all major works, especially those in Britain. As usual though, his question was not naïve; it was leading somewhere.

'You are very close in figure to her. But did you notice the little redness on the legs and buttocks of the original, Rebecca?' She had indeed, but she said nothing. Carlo went on, 'It is only a faint flush in contrast to the white of the back, but we must replicate this I think. You agree, signorina?'

She tried to sound noncommittal. 'I suppose so, if you insist on absolute veracity. I have some blusher in my bag.'

Carlo was deferential to Rebecca and not just because of her purchase of this portrait; her job meant that she could be very influential for his emerging reputation. Even so, it appeared he would not be diverted from his attention to detail.

'Yes I insist. But cosmetics will not create the true effect.'

Rebecca waited for him to continue. 'Come over to me, Rebecca. I think we can do this very naturally.' Adopting a languor she did not feel, Rebecca rose from the bed and came across to him, glancing at the easel as she did so. The unfinished portrait was brilliant; he had caught the graceful curve of her back and the folds and texture of the rich drapery beneath. So far her face, the lower half of her body and much of the background were only in outline. Even so, at this rate of progress she should be able to fit in another couple of days skiing before she returned to England.

Carlo had crossed to a tall cupboard against the far wall. As he closed the cupboard door Rebecca just managed to glimpse a small work in an ancient style.

'Been practising on the Italian primitives, Carlo?'

'It is an early exercise I did. I am ashamed for you to see it.'

Rebecca did not persist. She knew artists often hated to show juvenilia, especially if copied from much greater works.

Her attention was now drawn to the small leather paddle he had taken from the cupboard. Carlo handed it to her to feel and she slapped it against the palm of her hand. His smile was both cruel and irresistible. He caught her in his arms and kissed her lips, pressing her breasts against the rough wool of his sweater. How could Italian men always make you feel so horny? She suspected her skin would be flushed even without the paddle.

Carlo whispered, 'Lean over for me, amore.'

Rebecca obediently bent over a small table covered with paints and brushes. The studio's pleasant smell of linseed oil was more intense with her face so close to them. She felt the leather play over the skin of her bottom and legs. There was a pause before the paddle smacked the top of her left thigh. After another pause there was a series of light blows over the backs of her legs and the lower parts of her buttocks. They stung gently, but with each stroke she awaited the sharp pain of something harder. In frustration she urged him for more, but Carlo refused.

'No, we must have only a light pink for the portrait. Return to the bed now.'

Rebecca rose and kissed him hard; she was no longer in the mood for posing. 'Will you not join me there?'

Carlo took up his palette and brushes and sat on the stool by his easel. 'Let me paint a little more and then we'll see.'

It was pointless arguing with him when he was painting, so Rebecca returned to her pose. She had to support her head with her right hand, but at least her left was free. She began to masturbate quietly, and although her hand was hidden it was obvious what she was doing.

'I think you are a bad lady, Rebecca,' he said. 'What would Sir James do if he could see you?'

'I don't know. Perhaps he would spank me,' she

pouted, trying to make her voice as seductive as his.

'I will finish painting your bottom tomorrow - then it no longer needs to stay in such a perfect condition.' A rough change in his voice surprised her and she turned sharply towards him.

'No, Carlo. I can't have bruises when I go back to England.'

He cursed as the pose was ruined and replied shortly, 'They will be gone by the weekend. Your fiancé will not know.' He laughed at the look of alarm on her face and his tone became reassuring. 'Do not worry, Rebecca. I am an artist in these matters.'

Masturbation forgotten, Rebecca turned back to her pose. She could not tell how deep Carlo's cruelty went. Perhaps that was what made him so exciting.

That evening they took a short walk from his flat to a chic bar behind the Galleria. In doing so they crossed the vast space of the Piazza Duomo. She gazed at the enormous church, yellowy white in its night-time illumination. It was different to any other cathedral she knew; huge and squat and topped by a plethora of small spires, like an orderly collection of stalagmites.

As someone with a sharp head for business, Rebecca had spotted the anomaly of a poor artist living in a prime city centre location. Small though his studio flat was it had an expensive view overlooking the Duomo itself. Rebecca already knew from her friend that Carlo was from a humble background. She could not pry, of course, but his finances held a particular interest for her. It was evident that he was immensely talented, and she intended to try to contract him to her firm, so that they would handle his sales and exhibitions.

In the romantically lit corner bar they drank Bellinis and watched the passers-by. Through its glass sides they could observe upscale examples of Milanese nightlife moving to and fro through the Galleria Victor Emmanuel. Haughty women and suave men. Shades were much in evidence, even though it was night. Rebecca's eye followed one woman with interest. She wore a figure-hugging leather jacket and tight grey skirt. But it was her footwear that fascinated Rebecca: thigh high heel-less boots in clinging black PVC, as designed by Antonio Berardi. Someone walking without heels was a surreal sight. Although it seemed she should fall over, the girl actually walked gracefully. Fortunately she did not have far to go; a silver Ferrari pulled up by her side and the driver hopped out to open the passenger door. Carlo, too, was transfixed.

'Would you like to spank a woman wearing those boots?' she asked him playfully.

He flashed a winning grin at her. 'If the boots led up to your bottom I don't think I could resist.'

'You resisted me today.'

He shrugged. 'I must paint when the spirit is in me, amore.'

Rebecca saw that a woman would always be runner up in the race for Carlo's love.

After a while he disappeared, claiming a need to call his sister on a personal matter. Rebecca didn't have any reason to doubt him, but somehow she did. Underneath his dark charm, she was sure, lay an even darker nature. That they had grown so close so quickly was due to one incident, which had occurred almost as soon as they'd met.

A couple of Rebecca's skiing friends were also in the art trade. Carlo was an acquaintance of one of them and she had invited him over one night to hit the town with them. It was a forty mile drive to Bergamo, but he hadn't seemed to mind. Doubtless he was tempted more by the thought of loose English women than by developing his art world contacts. To the chagrin of the other girls Carlo had gravitated to Rebecca and they soon established a mutual attraction. Mid-evening, Carlo returned to his hotel room to fetch some photos of his work to show to her. After thirty minutes he still had not returned and the girls were restless to leave the hotel bar and find a nightclub. Rebecca needed to fetch her coat, so she said she would knock on his door in passing.

When she got to his door, however, she did not knock. From within the room she heard the sound of slapping, together with a woman's muffled yelps. Rebecca was familiar enough with these noises to know that some poor girl was getting her comeuppance. She was drawn irresistibly to enter the room, where she found Carlo sitting on the bed. A bare-bottomed maid lay across his lap, being firmly spanked. The girl was making quite a din in a restrained sort of way, but from long experience Rebecca knew she loved it. As soon as she saw Rebecca the maid tumbled off his lap, pulled up her panties and dashed red-faced from the room. Rebecca was left staring dumbfounded at Carlo.

'She came to turn down the bed, but I caught her prying amongst my things,' he said smoothly, a little flushed from his labours.

Rebecca did not believe him. She said nothing, but it didn't matter. It must have been easy to see the bright excitement in her eyes. He remained seated on the bed, looking up at her.

'Would you like to take her place, Rebecca?' he asked with a wicked smile.

'Not just now,' she replied. Not exactly an unambiguous refusal, she thought. She might as well have added, 'I'll take a rain check, thanks,' because the handsome devil knew she wanted to.

Rebecca liked what she saw in the photographs, and next day she allowed Carlo to take her back to Milan to show her the originals. He painted nudes with a classical beauty. As she examined them she formed the idea of sitting for him. The result would be a gift for James, for his eyes only. That was how she had come to spend much of her skiing holiday in Milan. She wasn't an expert skier by any means, so she didn't really mind.

Carlo returned from making his call, bringing her back to the present.

'Is your sister well?' she asked politely.

'Very well, thank you,' he replied, but his abstracted air suggested otherwise.

By the end of the following day Carlo had nearly finished Rebecca's face and body and no longer needed her to sit for him. He had taken a few charcoal sketches for reference and he would complete the portrait while she rejoined her skiing friends. At the weekend she would return and they'd fly to London together. Carlo had made arrangements to transport the painting as fragile cargo, once the paint had dried sufficiently for it to travel safely.

After the final sitting she stood before the easel, wrapped in a bath towel. Although she was not especially vain she gazed at the nearly finished portrait in admiration. Of course this work was much smaller than the original, but James would be delighted with his surprise wedding present. In a modern mirror the detail of the face had to be far more precise than the original, and Carlo had not failed her. Instead of being lost in complacent self-admiration like Venus, Rebecca looked out invitingly from the mirror towards the viewer. The woman in the picture might be aware of her own beauty, but the mischievous gleam in her eyes showed that she was more interested in its effect on an unseen man behind her. Her lips were parted in a slight but enticing smile. Carlo had perfectly captured a moment of feminine seduction.

He really is a genius, she thought. Like many young artists Carlo thought well enough of himself already, so Rebecca avoided praising him too fully to his face. Instead she said, 'I'm worried that James will think the look is too overtly sexual. He might even think I fancied the artist.'

'Tell him you thought only of him while you posed,' Carlo suggested. No doubt he had plenty of experience in advising young wives on how to deceive their husbands.

Rebecca, who knew that she needed no advice in how to handle James, simply said, 'That's a good idea, Carlo, I will.'

She went on, 'Actually, you've done a very good job.'

'More than good I think,' came his reply, and Rebecca smiled at the youthful mix of arrogance and honesty.

'Anyway, I think you deserve a bonus,' she said, moving closer to him and letting the towel fall to the floor. 'You know, I really did fancy the artist.'

'You should be faithful to your future husband.' For a moment she thought he was serious, but his actions spoke otherwise. He pulled her to him.

'I will be, once we're married.' Rebecca turned and rubbed her bottom into the erection beneath his trousers. 'But like Venus I can have affairs before then, can't I?'

'I don't think Sir James would agree. Like Vulcan he would be angry.'

'You're right. He'd probably demand to discipline me in some way. How do you think he would do it, Carlo?'

She led him over to the bed and kissed him. Then she knelt on top of it, leaning forward to rest her head on her hands. She watched him in the mirror as she waggled her bottom at him. She saw him pull the leather belt from his trousers and curl the buckle end round his hand. Still she watched as the belt was raised high in the air, time and again, and brought down with loud cracks across her buttocks.

Even though it felt good she knew she had to be careful. 'No bruises, Carlo,' she begged between strokes.

Carlo paused to take off his clothes, then in spite of her plea he took up his belt again. Soon she knew small welts and bruises would appear on her bottom, and began to flinch away from the strokes.

'Enough for the moment,' he crooned. 'Lie on the bed and I will soothe you.'

As he massaged the cold cream into her bottom it was not as soothing as he had suggested. He pinched and slapped the cheeks with strong hands. Now and then his fingers would probe between her legs, over the silky curls and between the sticky lips of her vagina. It was bliss, and Rebecca's moans must have told him she that could wait no longer. Without warning Carlo put his arm around her waist and raised her into a kneeling position. He entered her from behind and, gripping her thighs, pushed her forward and back along his penis. After a short while he withdrew.

She gasped in amazement. 'Wait! Not yet! Where are you going?'

He was over at the cupboard again and she begged in frustration. 'Beat me again later. Just fuck me now!'

'Oh, Rebecca, that does not sound like a well-bred English lady,' he mocked. 'I think you need to be taught a lesson right now. Vieni, amore.'

How can he hold back? she thought, but she obeyed, joining him at the tall stool by the easel. The items he had taken from the cupboard were lying on his paint table.

'Have you got a whole sex shop in that cupboard?' she asked in exasperation.

He smiled and bent her over the stool. He fastened her wrists in a pair of handcuffs, first looping the link around a crosspiece between the stool's legs so she could not get up.

'Vulcan's metal net,' he said.

For God's sake let's drop the mythological metaphors, thought Rebecca.

Carlo tied her ankles to a leg of the stool with a short leather strap. 'I have a slipper to punish the rude English schoolgirl,' he said.

Rebecca had already seen the slipper on the table and knew it was going to hurt like hell, especially after the belt. It was more like an espadrille, with a suede top and a thin rubber sole.

Well, you started this, she thought resignedly. You've only yourself to blame.

Carlo didn't show any compassion because it was her second beating in so short a time. He methodically slippered each buttock in turn, covering their whole surface but avoiding her legs. Rebecca gasped or yelped with each blow, depending on its strength. It did hurt, but she loved it; a paradox she had never tried to explain.

After twenty or so strokes he stopped and ran his hands lightly over her bottom cheeks. She could feel his erect penis bobbing against her, and a little fluid spilling from it. The large head pushed at her vagina. She had tightened up during the beating, so he held her lips apart with his thumbs and forced it in. Immediately her muscles relaxed. Holding her firmly by the hips, to keep the stool steady, Carlo thrust to and fro, gradually increasing the tempo. This time he did not back out.

After releasing her, Rebecca examined her bottom in the mirror. It was bright red and glistened from the cream. There were a few welts and small blue bruises, but nothing too serious. She looked across at him. He was standing naked, his erection only now beginning to fade, smiling at her whilst dabbing a little sweat from his forehead with a towel.

He was careful not to go too far, she thought. Professionally she was important to him, and James would be a dangerous man for Carlo to offend. So she had gotten off lightly. But she saw the sadism behind the smile, and she pitied any girl who fell into his clutches with no protection.

When she returned from the bathroom Carlo had his back to her. He was putting his toys away in the cupboard. From the doorway Rebecca had a better view of the painting inside. Cimabue in style, she thought, and not a bad copy as far as she could tell from a distance. She was surprised that Carlo had been uncharacteristically modest about it earlier. When he heard her he quickly closed the cupboard door.

'Fancy dinner, Carlo?'

'No, amore, I have to meet a friend for a drink tonight.'

'Another woman so soon? I feel used,' she joked.

'No, it is a man. I would ask you to join us but...' He shrugged and opened his hands to show that there were reasons he could not invite her.

'Never mind. My bottom's a bit sore to be sitting on hard barstools anyway.'

He smiled and kissed her and they left the flat together. They parted at the entrance to the building and Rebecca walked back her hotel in the Via Gesu. On the way she passed through the Piazza della Scala, glancing up at the monument to Leonardo. Across the road she saw the crowd milling at the entrance to the opera house, where the night's performance would soon begin.

At the Four Seasons she soothed herself in a relaxing bath, ordered room service, watched CNN and, at about ten, decided to call James.

In an altogether dingier part of town Carlo was discussing the transportation of the painting to England.

'I should prefer you not to move it until Monday,' he said.

'The sooner the better for you, my friend. Don't worry; I've crated paintings many times.'

His drinking companion was a tubby, bald man in premature middle age, whose fair complexion was beginning to show the blotches of alcohol abuse. He did not work for the shipment company whose name Carlo had mentioned to Rebecca.

'Does the Englishwoman know?' asked Bianchi,

casually.

'No, of course not,' said Carlo, drawing back from the other's pungent breath. He looked over to the bar and signalled for another coffee.

A woman in a red coat entered, bringing with her a gust of damp, chilly air. Bianchi shivered as it blew over his unprotected head. Fortunately for him customers were scarce tonight, so the door did not often open.

'My friend, sex games are one thing, but his interest in pain is more than recreational,' he said, sardonically. 'Neither of us wants to go there.' Behind his watery eyes was a penetrating gaze.

Carlo fell into thought, idly watching the woman take her coffee to the back of the room. He rested his elbows on the plain wooden table and came clean.

'She saw it from a distance. She thinks it's a copy I made at college.'

'But she knows about art,' persisted the other. 'It is a risk.'

Carlo shrugged. 'If she opens the crate, what will she find? Her own painting.'

His companion did not look convinced. Senor Bianchi was clearly the type who knotted his shoelaces twice.

'What if she remembers it when it comes to market?'

'She will never see it. It's a damaged minor work that will go straight into a private collection. There will be no publicity, no public viewings.' Carlo was becoming impatient with Bianchi's negativity.

Sighing mournfully, as one who has been given empty assurances a thousand times before, Bianchi accepted the spare key to Carlo's flat and left.

After the bald man had gone Carlo took his coffee to a table further back in the bar. The girl sat there, huddled in her red coat, hidden by the booth's fretwork screen. He kissed her on both cheeks and sat down next to her.

'How are things?' he asked anxiously.

'Not bad. They've moved me from the house to one of his clubs.'

'Which one?'

'It's called *La Pera*. It's the sort of place you would like,' she said, knowing a little of her brother's predilections. Carlo became agitated.

'Maria, I know it. It's not a good place for you.'

'Don't worry. I'm just a waitress. I'm not on stage,' she said soothingly. She didn't tell him that the floor manager was angling to put her into the show. For now the boss wouldn't let him, but if the money didn't come through that could change.

'I'm impressed you know it,' she said. 'It's pretty exclusive.'

He had visited it only once, as the guest of a wealthy businessman who was overjoyed by Carlo's painting of his wife. He had liked the entertainment well enough, but it wasn't the sort of place any man would want his sister to work.

'Do they treat you well?'

'Yes. The tips are really great. Sometimes I get pinched or a smack on the bottom, but I don't mind. It's a lot better than the house.'

He remembered the waitresses' uniforms. The corsets and fishnet tights tempted many a member's hand.

'I hate that,' he said with suppressed anger. 'And it's not your scene.'

Maria knew Carlo meant that she was not sexually submissive. But so far in her short life she had been forced to accommodate a wide range of men's tastes. 'Oh, I don't know. If I could find a nice guy I could take a good spanking now and then.'

'You are beautiful, Maria. Don't set your sights too low.'

She smiled at him. Carlo, she knew, was no angel, but he had always tried to be one to her.

Tentatively she asked, 'Do you know when you will have it?'

'I'm going to England at the weekend. Hopefully we'll sell them soon after that.'

She leaned across and kissed his cheek, her dark eyes bright with gratitude. The family resemblance in their faces was unmistakeable.

'I need to get to work. We open at ten.' She gave him a hug and left.

Restlessly smoking cigarettes Carlo took the long, cold walk back to his studio. This troubled Carlo would have intrigued Rebecca, who so far had encountered only his urbane arrogance.

Maria minded the gropes and pinches more than she had admitted to Carlo. In some ways the club was worse than the house. Few of the clients at the brothel had tried to hurt her; and if her bottom did occasionally come in for a drubbing it was in the privacy of a bedroom. Unfortunately, that night worse was to come.

At midnight a party of six or seven businessmen dressed in Zegna and Armani arrived. They were of various ages but all were well-oiled, no doubt from a sumptuous meal somewhere. December was an awkward time because Christmas parties meant that the customers were much more likely to be drunk and unpredictable.

Maria's heart sank when they were shown to a table serviced by her. There was an interval in the floorshow, so there was nothing to distract the men from teasing their pretty waitress. She stepped nimbly between their seats, on her ridiculously high-heeled mules, pouring glasses of champagne. With a fixed smile she steeled herself against their playful assaults on her bottom. But when someone poked his fingers into her crotch she staggered in disgust, her shoe went over and she flopped into a young man's lap. A good deal of the contents of a bottle of Dom Perignon flowed down his suit. He started back angrily, amid roars of laughter from his friends.

'She's in position, Filippo; you know what to do!' goaded one of them.

Filippo needed no further encouragement. He held Maria in place and slapped her behind. The slaps were gentle and she should have taken her mock punishment graciously; after all she had just soaked the man's jacket. She could feel the expensive wool cloth of his trousers against her, and a stiffening in his groin. If they had been alone it might not have been an altogether unpleasant experience, but she burned with embarrassment at being spanked in public, something which had never happened to her before.

When she scrambled to her feet Filippo released her readily enough. He smiled at her in a slightly inebriated way, while his table clapped and cheered. It could all have ended there, but Maria's injured pride pushed her too far. She slapped Filippo across the face. There were gasps from nearby tables, evidently glued to this bonus entertainment. As she stared down at Filippo, breathing heavily, she found him staring placidly back. It infuriated her that he seemed unfazed by her slap.

She had chosen a particularly bad night to break the club's code. The boss, who always treated her sympathetically, was absent. Her enemy, Bruno the floor manager, was deputising. Bruno was tall and thin, with slicked-back hair and sallow skin. He appeared at the table, gripped Maria by the arm and bundled her across the room into the boss' office. It was a dimly-lit, windowless room with worn out furniture upholstered in faded browns. A large oak desk stood opposite the door.

A waiter was sent to invite Filippo to join them. A few minutes later he returned with Filippo, who was now minus his jacket, which another waitress had taken to be sponged and pressed. Maria was made to stand meekly while Bruno launched into an elaborate apology.

It seemed that Filippo was a rising star in the

regional government of Lombardy, and Bruno was anxious to placate any ill-feeling towards the club that the incident might have caused. The entertainment at *La Pera* pushed the boundaries of legality from time to time, so through powerful connections and the judicious use of bribes they usually resolved any hiccups, but the club's license was a sensitive issue in some quarters.

Maria watched the young man from the corner of her eye as he listened patiently to Bruno's profuse flattery. At last Bruno turned to her, and ordered her to give her humblest apology.

Her cheeks were still hot with the injustice of it all and she made the mistake of protesting.

'But it was not my fault. It was the other man...' she paused, unwilling to say precisely what he had done, '...who pushed me.'

On hearing this Filippo was inclined to be magnanimous. 'Oh, I didn't know that,' he said, smiling at her. She sensed he was attracted to her. 'Well let's say no more about it,' he said briskly. He seemed not to want to waste any more of his night listening to tedious grovelling. Maria was beginning to warm to him. He was good looking in a studious way.

Needless to say, Bruno had other ideas.

'Waitresses here are expected to cope with friendly pats,' he rasped at her.

'Then I'm very sorry, sir,' she said, with such bad grace that Filippo was forced to laugh.

'Well you don't look it!' he said, grinning at her.

Maria blushed, a little ashamed at her sullenness when he had been so friendly about it all. She smiled at him and had just opened her mouth to apologise more sweetly when Bruno intervened.

'Perhaps you would care to give her something to be sorry about,' he said ominously. He took a long leather tawse from the desk drawer. Maria gulped. She suspected that Bruno had probably had this planned from the start.

'Shall we say twelve things?' added Bruno.

Filippo appeared to be stunned. He stared at the tawse and at Maria. The opportunity to whip her beautiful bum clearly appealed to him; she noticed the movement at his groin. She looked glumly at the floor, knowing her fate to be sealed. She wished she had been more pleasant to the young man after all.

'Oh, I don't think that will be necessary,' protested Filippo, and she looked up gratefully, liking him more and more.

But Bruno, as ever, was the killjoy. 'I'm afraid if you do not I shall have to discipline the girl myself.' His voice was heavy with sham regret. 'But I'm sure she would prefer it from you,' he added shrewdly.

Maria watched in horror as the young man's face brightened and he agreed. Bruno nodded to the waiter, who grabbed her hands roughly behind her back and held her down over the desk. It was completely unnecessary; by now Maria had accepted the inevitable and did not struggle. Before Filippo began Bruno straightened the seams of her tights, which had become twisted over the young man's knee. His bony hands brushed her bottom for a few moments and Maria felt sick with indignation and impotence.

Filippo gave her twelve swats with the tawse. Bruno made her count them and say thank you after each one. Although the blows were not harsh her humiliation reached new heights as she realised they would be heard at nearby tables in the club. Finally she was made to stand up and apologise again to Filippo, who nodded and told her she was forgiven.

Bruno asked the waiter to have two bottles of Dom Perignon sent to Filippo's table, with his complements. Filippo beamed and shook him warmly by the hand.

'You have been most accommodating over this matter, Bruno,' he said cheerfully. 'Signor Frapelli will certainly hear of it.'

Maria did not know who Frapelli was, but she supposed him to be a player who could further Bruno's interests in some way. That was Italy, she thought; the land that invented the concept of back scratching.

Filippo left, and Maria was about to follow him when Bruno called her back.

'Not so fast, young lady.'

It seemed her ordeal was not over yet. Bruno's cruel, pale eyes held her own while he pronounced further punishment. The young man had treated her with excessive leniency, which did not satisfy Bruno. He would give her a further twelve, this time on her bare bottom.

Under his direction Maria removed her corset. She hooked her thumbs into the waistband of her tights and pulled them down to her thighs, careful not to ladder them, and she was about to slip down her thong when Bruno said, 'Allow me.'

Her skin crawled as she felt his touch. Instead of holding the thong at her hips he hooked his thumbs in the front and back, and as he slowly pulled down he made sure the fingers of his right hand brushed her sex, and those of his left crept down the crack of her bottom. Maria shivered in disgust.

The waiter leered at her. They had never been friendly; she'd brushed off his advances soon after arriving at the club. He pushed her down again, pressing her bare breasts onto the scratched desktop.

'Your bottom is hardly coloured, Maria,' Bruno stated. 'We must change that.'

His strokes were twice a hard as Filippo's had been. Even more of the clients would be able to hear this time, she thought ruefully. But she took the blows bravely, counting and thanking him for each one as before, although by the last her eyes were shining with tears.

'It's a pity you do not suggest to the boss that you join the show, Maria. You would be a great attraction.'

She said nothing, but finished dressing and he let her go. Leaving the office with her the waiter insolently pinched her tender bottom. Bruno remained in the office, probably wanking off in the boss' bathroom, she thought.

When she resumed work her dark complexion was as flushed as the sore stripes on her bottom. She heard the sniggers of the customers as they ogled her behind, and through the fishnet tights her humiliation was visible to all She was furious at giving Bruno the opportunity to beat her and to use her as a pawn in sucking up to his patrons.

Chapter 3

Nicola's heart was racing as she lay in bed. She replayed the two scenes in James' study, trying to remember every word spoken and every stroke of the strap and cane. She felt more alive than she had for a long time. Eventually these thoughts naturally led her to recall the punishments her guardian had regularly meted out to her; what they had referred to as her 'confessions'.

Edward was not a handsome man, but he was attractive to women. From time to time he would have romantic dalliances, but had never come close to marriage. Even so, it had been the express wish of her parents that he be Nicola's guardian, in the event that they should both die while she was a child. Unlikely though that had seemed it sadly came to pass in the form of a car crash on a country lane. Nicola was seven at the time.

Edward was a Fellow at an Oxford college, and although Nicola was not academically inclined he always treated her as an intelligent girl, never making her feel inadequate by his superior learning. He raised her kindly, without ever smacking her; he told her later that she had been such a sweet tempered child there had never been a need. Nicola liked the compliment, but she knew there had been a childish tantrum or two over the years, although the confirmed bachelor had always taken them in his stride.

But all that was to change on her last day at school. Although she had to admit that it had been her fault, Edward's later revelations led her to wonder whether it would have happened anyway, just prompted by some other catalyst. However that may be, what actually caused it was her habitual weakness for exercising her sexual allure.

For some years Nicola had known that she was attracted to the seriousness and maturity of older men. She was turned off by the juvenile behaviour of boys. Unfortunately, older men were not readily available to her. Few attractive ones were still single, and in any case, dating a schoolgirl was taboo. Her efforts to flirt with her friends' fathers had brought at best the occasional hug or peck on the cheek.

That Friday evening she was no longer a schoolgirl. What was more, a few days earlier she had turned eighteen, so she was now a fully-fledged member of adulthood.

The end of year party was not until tomorrow, but a few of them had gone to the pub for a drink after school. A couple of Bacardi Breezers later Nicola had come home to find Edward in his study, at work marking university examination papers. A little alcohol made her bold. She undid a top few buttons of her white blouse, and revealed as much cleavage as she could.

'Can I get you anything, Edward?' she asked,

with a purr in her voice.

'I'm fine, Nick. Are you okay?' he asked, looking up. 'You sound as though you have a cold.'

'Actually, there was something I wanted to talk to you about,' she said, dropping the purr.

'Well I could do with a break from marking, so fire away.'

She went over to the desk and leaned against its edge in front of him. Her short pleated school skirt left plenty of bare upper leg. She moistened her lips, but said nothing.

'What is it?' he asked, puzzled.

'Can I sit on your knee? It's been ages since I did that.'

She moved quickly before he had a chance to refuse.

'That's because you're not eight any more,' he said, but he let her sit there and put an arm around her waist. She had flicked her skirt back so that her pantied bottom rested directly on his lap. As a regular cyclist he had firm thighs, and she wiggled her bottom against them.

'We're not really related, are we?' she asked innocently.

'You know we're not. Your parents were my close friends, but there was no family connection.'

She nestled a little further into his lap, one smooth thigh now resting on his crotch. 'Now I'm eighteen, are you technically still my guardian?' she asked.

'Why are you asking these questions?' His tone became wary.

'Because I wondered, now I'm an adult, whether you wanted...' she put her lips to his.

He recoiled immediately. 'What are you doing, Nicola?' He only called her Nicola when angry. 'Why are you behaving like a hussy?'

She blushed, and realised she should have expected this.

'I just wanted to kiss you,' she complained. 'What's wrong with that?'

'That's not the way you kiss a guardian.'

'Well I don't know these things. I need someone experienced to teach me.'

'You certainly need to learn a lesson,' he said, slipping her off his knees and pulling her facedown across his lap. Astonished, she began to wriggle and protest, but he told her sharply to stay still.

He started to spank her over her skirt, but that didn't last long. 'Pull it up around your waist,' he ordered.

She did so, revealing her white panties tightly stretched over her bottom, and he continued to spank her long and hard until her bottom burned. She wondered if he would take her panties down and spank her bare bottom, but he didn't. He did, however, slap her bare legs, almost down to the tops of her knee-high white socks, causing her to howl and bringing tears to her eyes.

After her first affronted struggle Nicola stayed in place, taking her punishment in a dignified way. Edward kept his left hand on the small of her back, but he had not needed to grip her tightly; the truth was that his stinging slaps excited her.

After the spanking he told her to stand facing the wall opposite his desk while he finished his marking. Her skirt was to be kept up, and she gathered it in front of her. A confusion of thoughts flooded through her mind: whether the red of her bottom was visible through the thin cotton of her panties; the pleasure of the tingling sensation which followed the initial pain; the joy of knowing that, during the spanking, she'd had his complete and utter attention. She imagined that he looked at her from time to time, and wondered if he found her toned legs and full young bottom sexually attractive. There had certainly been a hardening in his groin when she was across his lap. She did not know what he intended to do to her next but anticipation made her wet with excitement, so surreptitiously her hand slipped down the front of her panties and she began to rub herself.

All of a sudden he was at her side and saw what she was doing. She jumped, her face hot with embarrassment.

'I've finished the examination papers, but there is something else that needs to be given marks,' he said grimly, 'and this time I need a friend to help me.'

She was told to fetch the 'friend' from the tall cupboard by the bookcase. It was strange, she thought, that she had never known until now that it contained a school cane, and her eyes widened as it dawned on her what he proposed to do with it.

'Are you going to give me six of the best?' she

asked nervously.

'Six? No. Six is for schoolgirls. You are an adult now, and deserve an adult's punishment.'

Standing in the middle of the room Nicola was made to touch her toes. Her legs were to be kept absolutely straight and together. Edward lifted her skirt and lowered her panties to her knees. Hearing him swish the cane through the air was thrilling and frightening at the same time. Her heart thudded as he first rested it against her bare bottom, then let it play up and down her cheeks. This prelude seemed to go on for minutes before she heard the whoosh and crack of her first ever stroke of the cane, followed by the intense stinging she had known many times since.

Whereas the spanking had been bliss, the caning was not. At least not at the time. It was just as well the study faced the garden at the back of the house, or else her squeals might have attracted the notice of passing pedestrians. In truth they were a little theatrical, and Edward must have sensed it because although he made the first few swipes moderate, the rest were delivered with a full arm swing.

The beating was divided into two sets of twelve. Edward's instructions were given at the outset, and they remained the same for every subsequent punishment he carried out. She had to hold her position steady, and never try to nurse or protect her bottom. She was allowed to yelp and squeal but not to swear or blaspheme. She had to count each stroke and thank him for it, and for the duration of her punishment she must refer to him as 'sir'. All infractions of the rules would incur penalties, usually in the form of extra strokes.

Between the two halves of the caning he pulled up her panties and made her face the wall again. By now her skirt had been taken off, as well as her blouse. She stood in her white bra and panties, white socks and black shoes. To make sure she did not play with herself again she had to keep her hands on her head. Edward savoured his customary evening scotch and soda, and periodically came up behind her and ran his fingers under her panties and along the welts from the first session. His soft touch felt good, but when she gave a sexy little sigh to encourage him he gave each buttock a resounding smack.

It felt as though she had been there for half an hour or more when she risked a glance over her shoulder. Edward was still at his desk reading and sipping his drink.

'My arms hurt,' she whined. 'Can't I put them down yet, sir?' Nicola was finding obedience came naturally. Somehow his rules were comforting.

'You may, but keep them firmly by your sides.'

'Yes, sir.' Having won this first concession she tried for more. 'May I sit down, sir?'

'No. If you wish you may kneel, but keep your hands behind your back where I can see them.'

She knelt as directed, and ten minutes later he came over and told her to rise. She started to bend over in the centre of the room again, but he said they were going to her bedroom. As he followed her upstairs she felt his eyes glued to the movement of her bottom. When they reached her room he told her to put on her nightclothes; she would be going straight to bed afterwards.

'But it's only nine o'clock,' she grumbled, glancing at the clock.

'You will need your rest after this ordeal.'

'It's not so bad, I'm...' she started to say, before realising it would be better to keep quiet.

'There are still twelve to go,' he warned, 'and they won't be soft.'

Edward watched her undress. At her chest of drawers she hesitated. A mischievous idea had occurred to her, and she selected the baby doll nightie she'd bought to please an ex-boyfriend. It was transparent red chiffon with a matching thong. She pulled on the thong first, then quickly slipped the nightie over her head, but whatever reaction she had expected from Edward it was not the one he gave.

'Two extra strokes for impertinence,' he said, but did not make her change her nightwear.

He ordered her to kneel on the foot of the bed, knees together, bottom in the air. He lifted the nightie out of the way and delivered a good whack of the cane.

'One, sir, thank you,' she said.

'That was thirteen, Nicola. You'll receive another penalty stroke.'

Halfway through the set she started to move forward in anticipation of the cane hitting her, so Edward made her lie facedown on the bed. Pillows were put under her hips to raise her behind. He pulled the thong down to her thighs.

Hard strokes continued to stripe her cheeks until, by the last of the prescribed strokes, Nicola was crying and her hands were twisting the coverlet.

'Twenty-four, sir, thank you,' she sobbed.

Three penalties followed, cutting into existing welts and causing Nicola's body to buck and twist. Edward made the last such a cruel slash that she swore with the pain and her hands shot back to nurse her stinging buttocks. Accordingly, another two penalties were delivered, although rather lighter than the others.

After he had left her she rubbed soothing cream into her bottom. She went to bed in pain, but feeling strangely serene. She had a sense that she had reached a watershed in her life, but what she could not understand, until much later, was how Edward had resisted her advances despite her punishment being charged with sexual overtones. She went over the events of the evening, fantasising new endings while she masturbated.

Next day they had a long talk. Edward decided it was time to introduce discipline into her life in order for her to learn to control her flirtatious nature. He proposed a strict regime in which she would be thrashed on the first Sunday of alternate months; a total of six times a year. That would give her plenty of time to recover in between. These conditions would prevail as long as she lived in Edward's house. Yesterday's was the first, so the next would not be for two more months, but he emphasised that she should not expect every punishment to be as easy as the first.

Nicola listened, aghast. She was starting a new job soon, but she would not be able to afford to live elsewhere for some time to come. Yesterday's ordeal had excited her, but she was by no means sure that she wanted such agony on a regular basis. One chastisement was enough to fuel her fantasies for a long time. Nor had she found it in any sense easy, as he claimed it had been. In the end though, remembering how revitalised she had felt the night before, she accepted his terms and shook hands on the deal.

Under mountains of old books and papers in a spare bedroom there was a wooden whipping bench covered by an old sheet. As with the cane in the cupboard, Nicola was surprised she'd not discovered it at some point whilst growing up in the house.

They cleared the room together and Edward had it redecorated in claret wallpaper. Subdued wall-lighting was fitted, and the whipping bench was returned to take pride of place in the centre of the floor. A mahogany cupboard housed the implements he would use, together with any items Nicola wished to keep there. Because it had been a junk room the cleaner had never been asked to see to it, but just in case in a fit of domestic zeal she should one day do so, a lock was fitted. Nicola and Edward kept one key each. Nicola had to clean the room the day before her punishment. If she did not do a good job she could expect Edward to repay her appropriately. Although Nicola sometimes jokingly called it Room 101, it was usually referred to simply as the bench room.

The bi-monthly beatings soon became the sensual highlight of her life. Good looking boyfriends came and went with plenty of straight sex, but nothing thrilled her like those Sunday 'confessions' with Edward. Neither of them would make other engagements on those days. When Nicola was seeing someone she would avoid sleeping with them for the week following the beating, by claiming she was on her period. Any residual marks or bruises after then she would put down to bumps in the gym. But few boyfriends lasted long enough to notice any inconsistencies.

A regular routine was established, which was to change very little over the next three years. At seven o'clock in the evening Nicola would report to Edward's study, where she would find him at his desk. She would stand before him and catalogue her 'sins' since her last confession. She could vary the sins she chose to confess, although he required them to be based on real deeds. On one occasion she claimed to have committed no sins, but this made Edward beat her particularly severely for lying.

There followed her hand-spanking, which she received in his study, across his lap or over his desk.

In the bench room the instruments he used were grounded in English custom: the strap, the cane and, eventually, the birch. He favoured the latter particularly for penalty strokes, usually soaking it in salted water beforehand. The cupboard contained several of all types, in case one broke across Nicola's bottom, which it often did.

She was allowed to wear whatever clothes she wanted, and Edward encouraged her to experiment widely. In a sense it didn't matter because most, if not all, of them would be removed during the session, but he knew that different clothes could affect her frame of mind. If she chose to buy something especially for the punishment he would reimburse her. Skirts, shorts, trousers and uniforms were all tried, along with different forms of underwear. On one occasion she appeared naked except for high-heeled shoes. Impishly, another time she had bought a PVC jumpsuit, knowing it would be impossible to take off while she was strapped to the table. Edward solved the problem by carefully cutting out a rectangle from the suit, exposing her naked buttocks. Eventually, however, she came to settle on a particular combination of underwear which made her feel devastatingly sexy, and which she had noticed particularly aroused him. This was a classic satin corset and briefs, with which she wore suspenders, seamed stockings and matching court shoes. She had this outfit in three colours: black, white and red, which she alternated depending on her mood.

At first Nicola persevered in her attempts to goad Edward into reacting to her sexual advances. For example, she would deliberately rest her hand on his erection when she was climbing onto his lap. But in return he made her suffer by prolonging the spanking until her poor bottom was deep red, even before she had reached the bench.

The time she came closest to provoking a sexual response from him occurred before her first whipping on the bench. Edward had just taken off his jacket and was rolling up his sleeves. Instead of standing still, as she had been instructed, she stood some feet away from the bench and bent forward from the waist with her arms out, so that her fingertips just touched it, and spread her legs. Following her spanking she felt sexy and playful. She was naked and she dropped her head to see what her pert breasts and prominent nipples looked like hanging in this position. For a moment Edward's presence was forgotten as she narcissistically contemplated her own charms.

Abruptly her head shot up at his touch. She felt him standing by her side, running his right hand down the plain of her back. With his left he cupped and fondled her breasts. She was shocked and aroused at the same time. Was it going to happen now, she wondered?

'You remind me so much of Patricia,' he murmured.

She said nothing, but waited expectantly for his next move. His hands gently explored her upper body: her arms, her hair, her neck. Patricia had been her mother, but by now she was such a distant memory to her that it hardly seemed wrong to sleep with her old lover. Edward moved behind her. His fingertips caressed her bottom cheeks, the tops of her thighs and her sex.

'I loved every inch of her. I miss her so much.'

There was a crack in his voice. Nicola had never known Edward to cry, and she stood up, startled.

He was not exactly crying but his eyes were moist. She held him to her.

'I'm sorry I tempted you,' she said. 'I didn't mean to bring back painful memories.'

'You're a sweet girl,' he said, recovering his control and kissing her forehead. 'But I'm still going to give you some painful memories of your own,' he added, in a harder voice.

Her initiation on the bench proceeded, and Nicola left the room an hour later suitably chastened.

In the first couple of sessions in Room 101 the implements were restricted to strap and cane, but as she adjusted to the greater levels of pain Edward could move on.

The following spring the most fearsome object arrived. Or rather they had to collect it. Edward showed her how to make a birch rod. He told her they came in different forms, but he was particular about the type he wanted to use on her. She was to make three new ones each spring. She had to take straight rods from the young trees in his garden; both birch and hazel were present and she should use both. Four twigs, or rather small branches, were bound together in each birch. She had to select branches about three feet long that tapered to half a centimetre in thickness. After clearing the leaves they were tied together with string and soaked to straighten them. Once they had dried a handle was made by using a strong rubber tape to bind them at one end.

This year she made three more in the hope of finding someone to use them. No longer having access to Edward's garden she spent a walking weekend in Scotland. In wild forests near Bonar Bridge she was able to find suitable trees far from prying eyes.

Her first few strokes of the birch rod had seemed no worse than a severe caning, but its cumulative effect soon kicked in. The pain had a shattering intensity unlike anything else. The uneven wood left her skin scratched and speckled, although it soon healed. It was certainly the punishment she feared the most, but Edward had made sparing use of it. She was always bound to the bench to receive the birch, because it soon became evident that otherwise she would lose position with almost every stroke, and the extras would be endless.

After her sessions she rubbed cream into her punished skin. Nicola would have liked Edward to rub the cream in for her, but he would never do that. She assumed that it had always been the immediate precursor to sex with her mother, and he wanted to keep that memory sacred to her.

While the secret side of her life was exciting, her day to day work was not. Nicola had always preferred sports to academic pursuits. Physically she had always been able to push herself to new limits, but with deskwork she was lackadaisical. Edward often tried to boost her confidence by demonstrating how intelligent she really was, but she found it hard to keep her mind on the task in hand long enough to get very far. Later she discovered that a child's ability to concentrate was determined in the very early years of life, so she knew that it was not Edward's upbringing that had failed her in this way.

The result was that she left school with poor A-levels, which meant the jobs for which she could apply were monotonous. Her timekeeping was atrocious, oversleeping after late nights out, and figured often in her sin list at confessions. It resulted in several office jobs being lost. Her saving grace was that she interviewed well and, of course, was highly attractive to male managers, so she usually landed a new job quickly enough.

Once she had thought of proposing to an office manager that he use corporal punishment instead of sacking her, but it was not a practical idea. It was hard to keep secrets in large organisations, and the fall out could have brought embarrassing publicity. Besides, she knew that most men would view such a proposal as an invitation for sex, and she had no intention of becoming a slut.

Nicola could see that her feckless career hurt Edward. Once he became ill, fretting for her future without him. Eventually he talked his friend, Sir James Hammond, into hiring her. James and Nicola had met a few times in Edward's company. Although she liked his crinkly eyes and chiselled face, she had never tried to flirt with him. He had always been rather distant and she thought he might be a snob. At first she wasn't keen on the idea of working for him, but she agreed to it for Edward's sake.

Perhaps because he wasn't her parent, Nicola loved to spend time with Edward as a relaxation from her hectic and boozy social life. He was a civilised man with many friends. When they were in the company of others she would often make playful references to their secret. Inevitably she would refer to him as Edward the Confessor. At the tennis club, when they played on opposing sides in mixed doubles and she lost, she would tell the onlookers that he had given her a jolly good spanking. Edward's sangfroid gave nothing away, but her sassiness was added to the list of the sins to be redressed at her next confession.

When he died of pancreatic cancer she felt orphaned anew. But this time there was no second Edward to comfort and take her under his wing.

Chapter 4

They were cruising smoothly at eighty along the M40. A wintry sun shone on a landscape whitened by rime. Her side of James' large saloon was as warm as toast, and a gentle heat from the cream leather seat soothed her convalescent bottom. On his side of the car the climate control was set much cooler, but Nicola could luxuriate in her own cosy space. James drove sensibly, but it was pretty clear that the Audi accelerated twice as quickly as the draughty sports car of which her ex had been so pathetically proud.

She smiled to herself, recalling how James' eyes had surreptitiously followed her around the study that morning as she filed away books and papers. Tuesday had found her energetic and businesslike.

He, in contrast, had seemed a little lethargic, but fortunately a call from a dealer in London galvanised him. The dealer had acquired a rare painting which he thought James would like; he expected a lot of interest in the work and recommended James to come to the gallery as soon as possible to see it. So James decided to drive up that afternoon and stay overnight, rather than struggle home through the evening rush hour.

He had asked Nicola to book him a suite at Claridge's. If he was interested in the painting he said he would view it again the following morning before he left, so he might not be back until the afternoon. But as he was about to return to his study he stopped. She'd looked up from her desk expecting further instructions, but James shyly asked her if she would like to accompany him, almost as if asking her for a date. He said she could take dictation in the car, so it would really save him some time. They could do a little sightseeing and then have dinner. Or if she preferred she could do some late night Christmas shopping on her own. Surprised, she had flushed and accepted like an excited schoolgirl.

'Good. Well, book an extra room then. We'll stop at your flat on the way for your overnight bag.' Nicola was pleased. She knew that stuff about dictation was a fib. He had a dictaphone he used in his car often enough and she could have been doing work at the office as well. Not much time saving there, then.

Anyway, a short stint at dictation was over and she could relax for the remainder of the journey.

Rather sheepishly he said, 'I'm glad you seem so well today. I wasn't sure if we should go ahead tomorrow if you were...'

'I feel great. No lasting damage.' He looked so relieved she could have kissed him. 'Would you like to see?' she added cheekily, then laughed at this dry response.

'Better keep my eyes on the road. Maybe later.'

After this intimacy she felt able to push their relationship along a little. She looked across at the sensitive lines of his profile as he concentrated on the road ahead.

'Could I call you James from now on?' she asked hesitantly. 'Sir James is a bit formal.'

He seemed surprised but replied eagerly enough. 'Of course, yes. You must.'

'And my friends call me Nick,' she went on, wondering if he would think her too forward, presuming on his friendship.

'Is that because you're a little devil, Nick?'

'Perhaps. But you're beating the devil out of me, aren't you, James?'

'Well, fortunately today's a rest day, so the discreet hush of Claridge's won't be broken by the thwack of my strap hitting your lovely backside.'

She regretted a little changing out of her miniskirt at the flat. A good show of leg now might have produced an interesting result. She knew James thought her clothes too skimpy at work; that was partly why she wore them. But she hadn't wanted to embarrass him at a posh hotel. Like many older men he probably felt uncomfortable with girls who showed too much bare flesh in public, even though they liked it well enough behind closed doors. Still, she could see that she'd impressed him by changing into a dark grey skirt suit. The skirt came not too far above the knee but was still close-fitting and sexy. Beneath it she wore natural sheer tights.

In her warm cocoon Nicola soon fell asleep and dreamt that she was proudly introducing James to her former boyfriends. One of them, Kevin, asked if James was her father and she slapped his face. Then James fenced against all the boys and she cheered him on. Instead of swords they used school canes. In her dream James was an expert fencer. She felt horny just watching him. He lopped the top of Kevin's silly spiky haircut and left all their boyish faces with welts and bruises. They slunk off and left James kneeling over her, asking if she wanted him today.

She awoke with a start as they turned off Park Lane onto Upper Brook Street. James was glancing down a little anxiously, repeating, 'Are you okay?' He said that she seemed to have been having a pretty wild dream. She was lying back in her seat, but straightened up with a horrified squeak when she found her skirt had ridden up. She had a worrying feeling, too, that her hand had been between her legs while she dreamed. What would he think? She blushed, fumbling at the side of the seat for the electric buttons which raised it upright. She barely had time to straighten her skirt and regain her composure before they were drawing up in front of the hotel and a top-hatted doorman was opening the car door for her.

With his hand in the small of her back, James gently guided her through the main doors. Now she had recovered he seemed amused rather than annoyed with her.

'Sorry,' he said, 'that may have been my fault. I put the seat right back to help you sleep more comfortably, and you just seemed to slide down and catch your skirt somehow. Can be very slippery, this leather.'

'I'm sorry I dozed off at all while I was supposed to be working.'

'Oh, don't worry. Cold weather and a warm car always make me sleepy, too. That's why I like to keep my side cool when I drive.' He was being very nice about it, adding, 'Wherever you were, I wish I could have joined you. It sounded like fun.'

She didn't have time to reflect on the meaning of this cryptic remark before they arrived at the reception desk, where James was treated like minor royalty. After the receptionist had checked them in the duty manager led them first to Nicola's room. On the way he smiled politely at her, whilst asking James if his welcome return to the hotel was for business or pleasure. James said he expected it would be both, since staying at the hotel was always a pleasure. It seemed to be a big day for ambiguity.

Half an hour later James came to collect her and they left for the gallery. Darkness had fallen and the late afternoon streets were filling, as the home time exodus began to spill out into crowds of Christmas shoppers. The gallery was just off New Bond Street, a few minutes' walk from the hotel.

Its plush, dimly lit interior could be seen from the street, somehow managing to be both inviting to those with money and forbidding to those without.

The dealer greeted James unctuously and led them to a secluded alcove where a solitary picture hung on the wall. It was believed to be thirteenth century Italian, probably Florentine school, possibly by Cimabue. Apparently that was as exact as the dealer cared to be. Nicola had not heard of Cimabue, or of the Florentine school for that matter, and on this showing she didn't regret it. The painting looked every one of its seven hundred years of age. Against a gold background Mary sat in a black robe. Nicola took the grimy, doll-like figure climbing on her lap to be the infant Jesus. What remained of two angels looked on demurely from the corners.

Nicola could sense James was interested, so she left the two men to talk in serious undertones while she looked at the other paintings hanging in golden frames on the olive-green walls. The place had dark furnishings and an oppressive air.

Eventually James concluded his business and they were back on the street.

'Well, did you buy it?' she asked with interest.

'No. I said I'd think about it. I'm not happy about the attribution.'

'How much was it?'

'Likely to be twenty to twenty-five thousand.'

'No! But it's damaged!' She couldn't believe that he would even consider spending so much on that tatty piece of wood.

'If it were in decent condition it would be in a

major museum somewhere.'

Another aspect of the money occurred to her. 'That's about the same as...'

He didn't reply, and after a moment she asked, 'You didn't not buy it because I lost you that money?'

'Don't be daft, Nick. And speak English.'

She was being daft; from her work as his secretary she knew he had considerable wealth. But somehow she liked the familiar, casual way he reproached her. It made her feel less like an employee, more like a friend, or even a daughter.

They walked in companionable silence in the direction of Piccadilly, passing the expensive jewellers and fashion shops of New Bond Street. The warm glitter of gold and diamonds was enticing in the dark winter afternoon.

James hailed a black cab. 'I can see you're not impressed by Italian Primitives,' he said. 'It may be best to start with something more accessible.' She had no idea what he meant, but as he climbed in the taxi after her he told the driver, 'The National Gallery, please.'

They entered the Gallery from Trafalgar Square and turned right into the East Wing. James walked quickly through the rooms with Nicola in his wake. One or two of the paintings they passed she recognised from greetings cards or posters, but James did not stop for them. As they passed Van Gogh's Sunflowers at a brisk pace she was beginning to call out, 'Oh, I've seen that one,' but he was already past it and into the next room. It seemed he was more interested in the ones she hadn't seen.

At last he began to walk more slowly and stop in front of particular paintings. They would admire them together for a minute or two and then move on to another room. She realised he did not want to look vaguely at every picture in every room but specifically at a few he loved, for it was soon evident to her that he did love them; the intensity in his eyes and his straightforward but revealing comments told her that. She looked at these pictures with heightened curiosity because of it.

Her work for James had brought Nicola into contact with small works of art, but here was something of a higher order. For a start, she hadn't realised that many paintings were so enormous or in such vibrant colours. James did not say a great deal; the occasional comment about the artist's life; the look he'd captured on his sitter's face; the meaning of a small detail in the scene that Nicola might not have noticed. At some paintings he said nothing at all, leaving her to read the cards at the side and absorb them.

An hour passed very quickly as they moved through the East and North Wings. Amongst others, they had stopped at a marvellous reclining nude Venus, at a moving self-portrait of Rembrandt as a sad old man, and at a haughty pair of young Cavaliers dressed in satin and lace so lifelike she could almost feel the touch it. Nicola was starting to have an inkling of why people thought paintings were so worthwhile.

From their teenage years, Nicola and her friends had shown a healthy lack of respect for art as one of the grand totems of the world of their elders; whatever was shown them they acted as if they'd seen it all before. But here, forced to confront so much awesome beauty, she realised that she had not really *seen* art before. Her eyes had never lingered long enough to make the connection with the painting. Now she felt as though she were acquiring a new skill, or had awakened a part of her brain that had been dormant.

In the excitement of her discovery she began to make James stop at paintings that took her eye. To her great surprise he knew a lot about those as well. A deeper feeling for him was dawning in her. She had been sexually attracted by James the mature, assertive and wealthy man; now she could see something of his emotional character.

Nicola craved some physical contact to give expression to this newfound empathy. In the West Wing she noticed the unselfconscious way in which a student in torn jeans hugged his pretty girlfriend, while she giggled at yet another sexy portrait of Venus. But she had learned from her guardian that the code for public displays of affection was stricter for those of James' background. The large open rooms offered no privacy for them.

Their route seemed to be taking them back in time. Having walked along a passageway and past a wide staircase they entered the Sainsbury Wing. This, the newest part of the Gallery, housed the oldest paintings. She gazed at two small complementary portraits of a middle-aged burgher and his younger wife. They could almost be James and her, she thought, amazed that the brushwork just inches away had been set down nearly six centuries before.

She suddenly noticed that James was looking at her, not at the painting. He smiled and said, 'You don't need any special education to appreciate art; just intelligence and imagination. I think you've got plenty of both.'

She blushed at his compliment. Today he had made her feel a strange combination of innocent little girl learning afresh about the world, and perceptive adult able to think for herself, and she was grateful.

The rooms were now relatively empty and she looked at her watch to find it was almost ten to six. 'Don't worry,' he said, 'we've nearly finished, but we shouldn't miss the Leonardos.' He led her back the way they had come. *The Virgin of the Rocks* hung in a room near the entrance to the wing. He said very little about it, for it was plain that, in spite of looking highly anaemic, the faces had a timeless beauty, like that of no other artist.

Nicola was surprised to find that the second Leonardo wasn't a painting at all and was kept in a dark and tiny room behind the first. With so few people left in the Gallery she realised with a quiver of pleasure that, in this secluded space, she would finally be able to kiss him. Deliberately loitering until the other occupants had left the little room, she turned suddenly to face him.

'James, I want to thank you for today.' She put

her arms round his neck and pulled him to her. He was surprised, but he responded affectionately and they kissed. Then she turned and backed into him, taking his arms and making him pull her close while she looked at the charcoal drawing. She felt his cheek resting against her hair. After a few minutes an elderly man entered and looked a little embarrassed to see them, so they left.

In the taxi back to the hotel she sat close to him and held his hand. She planned to make love to him that night and was wondering how best to bring it about.

That evening they dined in the restaurant at the hotel. Nicola was intimidated by the formal service, but the restaurant was so busy she could feel part of the crowd and need not be worried that people would look at her and think she was out of place. On the other hand the atmosphere was far from suitable for the intimate one-to-one she wanted.

The food was immaculately prepared and presented. The wine was lovely; the name on the label vaguely familiar and she guessed it was astronomically expensive. James was attentive and told her some amusing tales about the art world, but in a slightly distant way. Nicola suspected that he was thinking of Rebecca and feeling guilty about their embrace at the Gallery.

After dinner she asked to see his suite, on the pretext that this was her first visit to Claridge's. Alone with her he seemed a little nervous of a repetition of the earlier intimacy. He avoided touching her as he briefly showed her the rooms, which were furnished in the Art Deco style.

'May I stay awhile?' she asked. 'It's still too early to go to bed.'

'Shall we go out for a drink?' he suggested.

Perhaps he was looking for an escape route, but that was not her plan. 'No, I like it here. It's peaceful after the bustle of London. I'd like a drink though.'

While James rummaged through the contents of the mini-bar Nicola took off her grey jacket and sat primly on the sofa. She sat with her knees together and hands in her lap, and rather gave the impression of a young schoolteacher in her grey skirt and white blouse. James poured brandies for them both, but instead of joining her on the sofa he chose to sit in the armchair. Given his coolness she was not sure how to proceed. Should she ask to use the bathroom and return dressed only in her underwear? The problem was, if he rejected her then she would ruin their growing intimacy and it would be impossible ever to try again. She decided to feel her way a step at a time.

'I didn't mean to embarrass you in the Gallery.'

'It's okay. You didn't.'

'I just wanted to show my appreciation. It just happened, really.'

He did not reply, just continued to look at her with grey, thoughtful eyes.

'Do you find me attractive, James?'

'You don't need me to tell you you're beautiful,' he replied evasively.

Beautiful, she thought. She liked that word.

'Since Uncle Edward died,' she ventured, 'I sometimes feel I need someone to turn to for guidance. It's easy to drift when you're young, isn't it? You know, just go with the crowd, have a good time, but not do anything very worthwhile.'

'Yes, I know. I did a little drifting myself at your age.'

'That's why I think that this...' she paused, 'this punishment will do me good. Help me focus on my job more; be a better PA for you.'

'Mm. Well you arrived early this morning - that's a first,' he said dryly.

Nicola laughed. 'It just shows how effective the cane is as a management tool.'

For a time they sipped their drinks in silence. Then, casually, Nicola said, 'Maybe you ought to check my bottom has recovered enough for tomorrow's session. This morning you said you would.'

'Did I? I thought you said it was fine.'

'It feels fine. But you've probably got more experience to judge.'

He coloured a little at that, and then replied, 'It would make more sense to look tomorrow evening.' This was so obviously correct that Nicola could only agree.

'I suppose it would.'

At least she had caught a glimpse of movement beneath his trousers, so some progress was being made. She just needed a little more time. 'It's warm in here. Aren't you hot in your jacket and tie, James?'

'A little. I was going to take them off when you

left.'

If that was a hint to go she was going to ignore it. 'I don't mind. I'd be sorry if you felt you couldn't relax with me.'

'You're right. I shouldn't stand on ceremony; Rebecca says it's a weakness of mine.' He got up and took off jacket and tie. Nicola glanced quickly towards his groin.

Yes, definite signs of life, she thought, and if the mention of his fiancée was another hint to back off she was going to ignore that, too.

They sipped their drinks in silence again.

'Actually, James...' Nicola hesitated and he looked at her expectantly. She continued slowly, eyes fixed on the table. 'I would prefer to know tonight whether the next punishment will be tomorrow. It's just that...' another pause. 'It's just that, if it isn't, I'll probably go out with some friends and I need to let them know.' She was still not looking at James but she could sense a tension in him. Nice one, she thought, that was a pretty good excuse on the spur of the moment. For the clincher she turned her hazel eyes on him, limpid with unshed tears.

James did not reply at once; he seemed to be struggling with himself. Perhaps he had seen through her; after all, he was an experienced man. Yet she knew that most men could be fooled by female tears, especially those that led them where they wanted to go anyway.

'I understand. Yes, of course. I should really have thought of that.' Usually so confident he was stumbling a bit now.

She waited, looking at the table again.

'Maybe I had better take a look now,' he said at last.

'Thanks, that would be great. I'll just use the bathroom to take my skirt off; I don't want to get it creased again.'

'Call the valet service; they'll have it pressed for you.'

Valet service? Nicola thought. This was getting exasperating. Why the hell couldn't he just let her seduce him without throwing out all these diversions?

'It's okay,' she said. 'I'll call them later from my room.' She smiled sweetly and rushed to the bathroom before he could think of any more suggestions.

When she returned James was still in his chair but he had topped up the drinks - definitely a good sign. Nicola held her arms in front of her breasts, hands on shoulders. 'I don't want to embarrass you but I took off my bra too. Yesterday you made me take it off so I thought...'

He didn't reply.

'Is that okay?' she asked. He nodded. They were watching each other closely now. She saw his eyes fall to her breasts as she took her arms away. She glanced down too, at a large erection in his trousers. Going good.

Nicola had a sip from her drink then took something from her bag and moved over to James' chair. She stood with her back to him, legs firmly together. This evening rather than a thong she was wearing knickers of white lace which nearly covered her bottom cheeks; and she had left her tights on. To see her bottom properly James would have to take down both.

After a slight pause she felt his fingers hook into the waistband of the tights and firmly pull them halfway down her thighs. But instead of sliding her panties down he held aside the lacy material, revealing one buttock at a time. She felt his fingertips run over the surface of the cheeks. He squeezed and patted them gently. The welts had gone completely; just the odd red blotch and one or two tiny bruises remained. His fingers moved down to examine the tops of her legs. Ever so slightly she changed her stance to part her legs. His fingers probed between them and lingered on the crotch of her panties. He must have felt the wetness there, but he just straightened the knickers and brought her tights up again.

'Seems fine,' he said, giving her bottom a sharp slap.

'Ow!' exclaimed Nicola. 'It's still a little sore,' she said. 'I've been rubbing cream into it.' She turned and held out a tube of lotion. 'Could you rub some in for me? It's easier if you do it.'

He looked her in the eye for a moment, but before he replied she said in a businesslike way, 'It would be better on the sofa. Then I could lie across your lap more comfortably.'

For an instant she thought he was not going to buy it, but he did. He moved across to the sofa and she immediately went over his lap.

'Oops, I've still got my tights on,' she said, pushing herself up. But instead of rising and taking them off she moved one hand to his erection and held it through his trousers. James said nothing, but he was breathing more quickly. Nicola unzipped him and pulled his stiff penis out over the top of his white boxer shorts. It was not the largest she had seen, but it was large enough. She slid a little off his legs and dropped her head to his lap. She licked the length of the rigid penis with the tip of her tongue.

'You really *are* a little devil, Nicola.' He spoke angrily, but that did not worry her at all; she knew he wanted sex with her. Her tightly clad bottom still rested within reach on the sofa and he gave it a stinging slap.

'Yes,' she gasped in pleasure. 'Spank me, James; you still owe me that from last night.' She took his penis into her mouth, her head bobbing as she vigorously ran her lips up and down its length. The thrill made his spanks haphazard, but they were heavy and frequent. Nicola gasped and bucked with each blow but she kept her mouth around him. James was close to orgasm and the spanking stopped, he gripped the seat of the sofa. Out of breath Nicola hurriedly rose and pushed down her tights and knickers. She bent forward over the chair seat with her legs apart and her bottom in the air.

As James rose and moved behind her his mobile phone rang. They could tell from the ringtone that it was Rebecca. Nicola begged him not to answer, but after a moment of indecision he did. Rebecca must have been able to hear he was still breathing heavily.

'I've just come up the stairs,' he said into the phone, standing with trousers round his ankles.

All that good work for nothing, thought Nicola, slumping in the chair with a muffled groan. With a look he signalled her to keep quiet, and she listened to his side of the conversation. It was pretty monosyllabic and he didn't ask much about what Rebecca had been doing. All in all Nicola thought Rebecca would guess that something was wrong, and she was not surprised to hear him say, 'Yes, actually I'm with Nicola.'

He handed the phone to her, and she sat up in surprise.

'Rebecca would like to talk to you.' She looked at him in puzzlement, but she took the phone and tried to sound as bright as possible.

'Hello, Rebecca. How's the skiing?'

Nicola listed attentively for a few minutes, with the odd word of assent, and then handed the phone back to James. While he spoke with Rebecca his eyes were hungrily following Nicola as she dressed. Before the call ended she kissed him on the cheek and left to go to her own room without a word.

Chapter 5

Alone in his suite, James mused on the chaos he was unleashing in his private life. He was still plagued by the memory of Nicola, bent over the chair begging him to fuck her, but he was determined not to masturbate for relief. Still less would he go to her room, where no doubt he would have been warmly welcomed. Rebecca's call at the very moment he was about to be unfaithful to her had been a sign. He needed to bring the relationship with his secretary back under control.

On the whole James thought the phone conversation had ended well. He doubted Rebecca suspected anything was amiss. He'd explained how he had needed to come to London and simply invited Nicola on the spur of the moment, as a treat.

'A sort of staff Christmas party for the two of you,' Rebecca had said.

James was glad she was so understanding, but that did not lessen his sense of guilt. He knew where Nicola's conduct was leading and he should have nipped it in the bud.

The trouble was that he found the girl devastatingly sexy. It was impossible to resist the way she was complicit in her own punishment. Impishness and innocence alternated in her in the most sexually provocative way. From the moment she asked, 'Couldn't you punish me in some other way?' he was caught in her elflike spell. The lovely hazel eyes that could moisten in an instant; her sweet voice which quavered like a child's; the silky bob cut which fell about her cheeks when she meekly lowered her head; the youthful freshness of her scent. But most of all her beautiful body and delicious derriere. He wanted to hug her, spank her and make love to her all at the same time.

And yet he suspected that, in spite of this craving, his true love was for Rebecca. Although younger than James she was far nearer his own age than Nicola. Her work and interests were similar to his, and sexually they were wonderfully compatible. He tried to dampen his lust for Nicola by thinking of Rebecca.

They had met a little over a year before at a restaurant in Oxford. He had taken his mentally disabled cousin, Frank, out to dinner for a treat. Frank lived in a care home nearby. He was an attractive looking boy, at the difficult age of sixteen. All youths find it hard to cope with their emerging sexuality, but those with Frank's problems are simply unable to grasp what is happening to them. In the restaurant Frank had not been able keep his eyes off Rebecca's long chestnut hair.

Rebecca was dining with her mother at a nearby table and it soon became clear that she did not welcome Frank's leering attentions. James tried to distract him, but he'd fixed on Rebecca with the single-mindedness that typified his behaviour. Not even the arrival of his much loved steak and chips diverted him.

Just as James was considering crossing to the other table to explain the position, Rebecca swept over and started, quietly but heatedly, to put the rude teenager in his place. James tried to intervene, but she ignored him. Frank was dismayed and James could see in him the signs of imminent distress.

Later James always justified what he did next as actuated by concern for Frank, yet he never believed that to be the true explanation. Rather, it felt as if fate had taken a hand to change his life in an instant. And 'hand' was the *mot juste*. Rebecca was leaning against the table towards Frank, displaying a lovely bottom tightly clad in a white satin evening dress. On an impulse James raised his right hand and brought it down with a loud slap on Rebecca's behind.

There was silence across the restaurant and all eyes turned to their table. Rebecca shot upright with a comical look of astonishment. The silence was broken by Frank's high pitched laugh. As she heard it, James could see enlightenment dawn on Rebecca's face. He whispered quickly to her that Frank was a teenager with special needs.

The head waiter had hurried to the table and was in the middle of asking James to leave when Rebecca interrupted to say that it was all a joke and she had not minded at all. She immediately soared in James' estimation and he smiled at her gratefully.

James rather rushed the rest of their meal. There were disapproving glares from all quarters, with the notable exceptions of Rebecca and her mother. Although they threw several glances his way, they did not appear to be hostile.

He wrote a brief apology to Rebecca on the back of his card, giving it to the head waiter with instructions to deliver it after he had left. Both tables were to be charged to his account. He included a hefty tip for the disturbance. In addition, the waiter was to urge the women to select an expensive wine to accompany their desert. As he and Frank left James was amazed to receive a warm smile from Rebecca's mother. Rebecca herself coloured slightly and looked at her plate.

A couple of days later Rebecca called to thank him for his generosity and to apologise for any distress she may have caused Frank. He apologised in turn and she laughed, saying that she had been spanked by a man before but never by a total stranger. Thinking about this later, James realised that Rebecca had made a revealing remark and he wondered whether or not it had been intentional.

In comparison with the scene at the restaurant, their first date was a tame affair. Over lunch they discovered shared tastes in music and, especially, art. James occasionally dealt with the firm for which Rebecca worked, and she knew of his reputation as a respected collector with expertise in early Italian works. James listened attentively to her as she recounted her interests. Much later, Rebecca told him how his ability to concentrate his attention so intensely on her was something she loved. He never admitted to her that at that first date, while he'd been taking in her words he was dreaming about taking off her clothes.

For their next outing she suggested they take Frank out together for the day. It was a gesture of kindness that moved James. They went to a large amusement park, where Rebecca lavished attention on Frank. She was a natural at making him happy without letting him get over-excited. Naturally, it helped that the boy had a crush on her. As Frank slept in the back seat on the way home they talked more intimately. That night she stayed at his house. By morning, James had fallen in love.

Their first sex was a slightly fumbled affair. He was acutely aware of the ten year age gap and tried too hard not to disappoint her. Even so, they both sensed a strong physical attraction on which they could build.

The following weekend they had their first fight, and from then on their lovemaking became far more fiery. It started over a trivial compliment made by Rebecca about a colleague who'd had breast implants. They were relaxing on the drawing room sofa, reading the Sunday newspapers. Without looking up from his paper James made a scathing comment to the effect that sensible men did not want to caress bags of saline or silicon.

Rebecca immediately bridled. She pointed out that it was the woman's choice; that contrary to what James thought, men did like women with boob jobs; and that big breasts improved a woman's self-esteem. He responded that he thought women with oversized breasts looked practically deformed.

'Are you really saying that you would be happy with a woman with an A cup?' she asked, staring at him incredulously.

'Of course, if I were attracted to her,' he replied, equally surprised that she should think otherwise.

'Aesthetically her body might be far more beautiful than someone with double D breasts. Anyway, I've been out with many women with small breasts.'

'So I suppose you think I'm deformed?' asked Rebecca coldly. Suddenly they were in dangerous territory. Her tone of voice suggested that there was going to be a row no matter what he said. Since Rebecca was a perfectly proportioned thirty-two C, James did not see the logical connection between his statement and her question. He told her so a little testily.

'The logical connection,' replied Rebecca hotly, 'is that you're an old male chauvinist fart, living in the fifties.'

On reflection James had to admit to himself that his blatant honesty could sometimes be a little naïve where women were concerned. He cursed himself for having reached forty without learning to sidestep such traps.

Rebecca jumped up and looked down on him, flushed and breathing quickly. She was standing so close that her jeans brushed his leg. James remembered thinking it odd that the pants she had chosen for Sunday morning were so tight. Perhaps because it was early in their relationship she was not yet confident of her sexual attraction over him.

'Well I think I need a boob job, and I'm having one whether you like it or not.'

James had a favourite phrase which had sometimes been his escape clause from similar scrapes. It had always worked best when he was sexually aroused, as he was now, eyeing the skin-tight jeans.

'What you need,' he said, 'is some sense spanked into you, young lady.'

With that he caught Rebecca's arm and pulled her down across his lap. She shouted and struggled as he slapped the dark blue denim. When her T-shirt rode up, exposing her midriff, he put his hand in the hollow of her back and pushed her down firmly. Rebecca continued to throw her arms and legs about, but in a way which did not convince James that she wanted to escape.

She just doesn't want to be seen to give in too easily, he thought.

After a while Rebecca's wriggles ceased and she calmly acquiesced to his smacks. When he stopped and put his hand beneath her to unzip her jeans she lifted her hips to help him. He pulled the clinging material off her round pink cheeks, and slipped down her thong.

Mesmerised by her lovely bottom he delivered measured spanks for what seemed like an age. Each one brought an answering gasp from Rebecca. By the time he relented her cheeks were very red indeed. Looking at his handiwork, it occurred to him that after her initial protests had ceased, Rebecca said nothing. Not so much as an 'ouch' escaped her lips.

He pushed his hand between her legs and found his answer. Lifting her into his arms, jeans around her ankles, he took her upstairs to the bedroom. As they went she stayed silent, but she put her arms around his neck and rested her flushed face on his shoulder. Sunday mornings, he reflected, smiling, did not come any better than that.

In her room, Nicola was not asleep either. But instead of distant memories her mind was focused on the night's events. They had not panned out as she'd hoped, but the good news was that her tactics had been working. It was unlucky that the phone call came just when it did, otherwise she would probably not be alone in bed now. She had demonstrated without a doubt that James could be seduced; she just had to strike while his penis was still hot.

The obvious choice was tomorrow's session. Sooner or later during it she would end up almost naked, without any need for subterfuge on her part. That was half the battle. The other half was to get James naked too. It was not helpful if she had to urge him too eagerly to lose his jacket and tie. Tomorrow that would be harder to do; he would be in his study and may be wary of her advances after tonight. To help her she would prefer a less formal ambience. She didn't know, either, if Rebecca said anything in her phone call to deter him.

Rebecca! Nicola suddenly questioned the motive for her actions. Did she hope to supplant Rebecca and marry James? Probably not. Then why was she hurting the woman in this way? Rebecca could be brusque and haughty but she had never done her any harm. What Nicola was doing was wrong and she knew it. But sometimes when you wanted something you took it and ignored the consequences, for yourself and for others.

What she wanted was to discover what sex with a handsome older man was like. Edward had denied her advances, and rightly, she could see that now. No matter how she had tried to tempt him he resisted her. Once she suggested that she gave him a blowjob, because that would not really be sex between them. In response Edward unleashed six searing extras with the birch, and left her bound to the whipping bench in tears for an hour while she 'contemplated the impropriety of her proposal'. It all meant that, ultimately, her confessions had left Nicola unsatisfied.

But James was another matter. She had come too close to give up now. And after sex, would there be an ongoing relationship with him? Perhaps. One step at a time. She would see.

James poured himself another drink and continued his reflections. Rebecca's first caning had been another milestone in their relationship. Although he had already given her some stinging swats with a riding crop, the caning was far more severe, revealing her high threshold for pain.

They had been together for two or three months and she had given him plenty of reasons to spank her. Even when she gave him no reason, he sometimes put her over his knee anyway; or bent her over his desk, or a chair, or the bed...

Their lovemaking reached levels of delight James had never before found, and he believed Rebecca felt the same. Outside the bedroom they felt comfortable as a couple, whether they were in galleries, at parties or simply lounging at home. When he was alone, James was giving serious attention to engagement rings.

It was a Friday evening in early October. An Indian summer meant he was sitting in the garden nursing a gin and tonic when Rebecca arrived. By now she had plenty of clothes at James' place, so she had come straight from work, still dressed in a grey pinstripe business suit and dark blouse. He admired the high-waisted pencil skirt, which accentuated her hips. She sat down in a garden chair next to his and accepted a drink.

'I'll just have one, before I go and change,' she said.

For a while they discussed plans for the weekend, but he sensed there was something she wanted to tell him. Accordingly, he fell silent and waited.

'James,' she began sheepishly, 'there's something I need to own up to. I hope you don't mind.'

If I do mind you'll be over my knee in a jiffy, he thought, but said nothing.

'It's about the landscape you agreed to buy from us.'

Earlier in the week James had visited her firm's London gallery and agreed a price on a small seventeenth century Dutch landscape painting. Delivery had been arranged for the following week.

It so happened that the firm were trying desperately to cultivate a wealthy collector, Janssen, who specialised in Dutch art. When this potential client had enthused over James' landscape, Rebecca authorised its sale to him. Clearly she had thought that, being James' girlfriend, she would be able to coax him out of making a complaint.

James was horrified. His code of business had always been *dictum meum pactum*. He pointed out that if Rebecca were ever to do this to someone less understanding than James, the news would get out, and it could shatter her professional credibility.

'I'm really sorry,' she cooed, after he'd scolded her. 'I just thought with us being together you would do this for me as a favour.'

'I might have done, if you'd asked me beforehand,' he said angrily.

'Spank me. Then we can kiss and make up,' she pleaded.

'No. It's too serious,'

'What then?' she said, becoming concerned. 'You're going to make me get the painting back off Janssen! We'll lose his business for sure and he'll make a big fuss.'

'Exactly. And your professional name will be mud. But I'm not going to make you do that.'

Rebecca appeared very relieved.

'I'm so sorry, James. What can I do?' She sounded sincerely penitent, but James was not inclined to be too forgiving.

The gardener, who had been clearing out the greenhouse at the end of the season, had left a pile of unused bamboo canes on the path a little way from the French windows. Presumably he had meant to take them to the shed to keep for next year, but forgotten to do so. He tended to slink off as soon as he could on Fridays.

James had noticed the canes earlier. Now he anticipated a better use for one of them than to support next year's vegetable crops.

'What you can do is follow me to my study, and on the way in pick up a couple of canes from the pile over there.'

Rebecca's eyes widened in horror. He could see she knew what he intended to do. She started to object.

'Not that, James. Please. I had the cane once and it really hurts,' she whined.

At a later date James would be interested to know how Rebecca had come to be caned in the past, but at the moment he wanted to concentrate on the matter in hand. He ignored her appeals for mercy. 'Do as I say. Quickly,' he ordered.

Two minutes later Rebecca stood before the desk in his study, awaiting her fate. The canes were on the desktop. James intended to draw out her discomfort.

'Lift your skirt and show me your underwear,' he demanded.

The skirt fitted her tightly, hugging her bottom. It was not easy to lift. 'I'll crease it,' she complained. 'Let me just take it off.'

'If you keep talking back I'll double the number of strokes. Lift it up.'

She slid the skirt carefully up her legs, revealing the tops of her black stay-ups and a pair of French knickers in black silk. He told her to lower the skirt again and take off her jacket. Meanwhile he swished the four foot canes through the air and selected the one he preferred. With his handkerchief he wiped it clean of the dust from the greenhouse.

Rebecca folded her jacket over a chair and returned to the desk. He made her adopt the usual position: ankles together; straight legs, arched back. He smoothed down the skirt, which clung nicely to her curves.

When he announced her sentence of twenty-four strokes she gasped in protest. 'I'll never be able to stand that many!'

'I think you'll be surprised what you can stand when you have to.'

As it transpired they were both surprised how well Rebecca took her beating. With each crack of the cane she let out a small squeal, but kept her position well. He had given her eight on her skirt, eight on the French knickers and was finishing off with eight on the bare buttocks. With just four strokes to go she began to sway forward. He smacked her bottom and told her to be still, before finishing off with four juicy swipes.

At the end he admired the grouping of his final strokes, which had left eight thick, nearly parallel weals. He allowed her to rise, turned her towards him and kissed her.

'You are forgiven,' he said.

She kissed him back, while nursing her stinging bottom. Her face was hot and her lips moist. He praised her fortitude, but she groaned when he told her that at last he had found something to give his right hand a rest.

Previous plans were rearranged and they spent most of the weekend in passionate lovemaking.

As James was drifting off to sleep he recalled a further episode of their life together, perhaps the most important day so far in his life. It was the day he became engaged to Rebecca. After much searching he found the ring he wanted - a five carat emerald cut diamond set in platinum. He'd felt that she had a sense of expectation that weekend and he wanted to surprise her by choosing an unlikely time to propose.

They were out riding and had just finished a fast canter across the hillside. Still mounted, they admired the marvellous view of the Thames winding through woodland below them. When James climbed down she looked puzzled. He said there was something in the grass beneath her horse. She sat patiently, controlling the horse as he came near. He went down on one knee, appearing to look in the grass, and when he came up he held out the ring and spoke a few prepared words. It was the only time he'd seen tears in her eyes. They must have been tears of joy, because her reply was ecstatic.

In the following weeks sex was passionate and punishment free. But Rebecca must have tired of her genteel treatment, because three weeks later she brought him an engagement present. He was stunned to find in the box the painting that had been sold to Janssen. His face lit up with happiness.

'But how did you get him to sell it?' he asked.

'It turns out he's a romantic at heart,' she replied, delighted at his reaction. 'And of course, he made a small profit on the deal.'

Beneath the painting was some tissue paper, and when he removed it he found some very raunchy underwear for Rebecca, and a black leather strap.

Chapter 6

James had told Nicola that he wanted to leave the hotel at six the next morning to get out of London before the worst of the rush hour. With most of the traffic coming into the city there were few delays and they were on the motorway in well under an hour. They drove in silence. Nicola, it seemed, seldom saw this early hour of the day and she was sleepy, but James' mind was very active. He pondered how this relationship had moved so far in just two days and, more importantly, what he should do about it. His thoughts were interspersed by distracting visions of Nicola in a variety of submissive poses.

At eight o'clock he was waiting in the living room of Nicola's flat in Marlow, while she dropped off her bag and collected her sports kit. She seemed to be taking an age about it. Wednesday was normally a gym night for her, but since her second punishment was due today James had agreed that she could use the small gym at his house, to avoid missing her training.

He wandered restlessly around the untidy room,

touching items of clothing she had carelessly discarded. Glancing through her collection of CDs he was taken aback to find the familiar range of popular music interspersed by a few classical albums. On reflection he knew he shouldn't have been surprised; she was an intelligent girl raised by a university don.

When she appeared from her bedroom the reason for the delay was apparent; she'd changed her clothes. She was now wearing black pants which fitted like a second skin, showing every contour of her legs, hips and bottom. As yet she had on no top, but she wore a black bra.

She came up to him coolly, saying, 'I just wanted to check these are okay for office wear. They're not jeans.'

She was taunting him for grumbling about her jeans a few weeks before.

God, she is impudent, he thought. She really has it coming tonight.

She noticed a Rachmaninov CD which absentmindedly he still held in his hand, and at once her pert manner changed.

'That was one of Edward's favourites,' she said sadly.

'It's beautiful music. Do you like it, too?' he asked.

'Yes, but I can't listen to it very often,' she mumbled. She turned away quickly and disappeared again. He knew she was hiding real tears, and he regretted his unkind thoughts a few moments before. That was the way it seemed to be with Nicola: one minute he wanted to spank her and the next to comfort her.

While she finished dressing James looked at the few pictures in the room, and a wedding photograph of Nicola's late parents caught his eye. The newlyweds stood on the lawn before a large Georgian house, presumably where their reception took place. The big 80s hairstyles looked absurd now, but their happiness still shone through. Next to it was a photo of a young Nicola on holiday with Edward in front of a Roman ruin. These three dead people were all the family Nicola had ever possessed. Deep in his melancholy thoughts he suddenly noticed her at his elbow. He guessed she might have been there for a few seconds.

'Ready,' she said, smiling brightly, but her eyes still glistened.

Back at the house in Henley, James found it impossible to concentrate. Nicola seemed to have an endless amount of filing to do around his study, much of which involved stretching and bending in her tight trousers. When questions arose she would stand close beside him, leaning over the desk while he read the document. He could smell the cleanness of her hair and knew that if he turned his head his lips would be inches from hers. The desire to move back his chair and fling her across his lap was almost too much to bear. His hand itched to make contact with the well-stretched black material and the supple flesh beneath it.

At midday he went through the French windows onto the lawn for some respite from his erection, which had been more or less present for over an hour. It was a crisp, clear day and he scrunched the frozen grass as he walked down to the riverside. Whatever the weather, rowers were always in action. He watched a couple of fours glide by, blades wielded by strong young men moving in perfect unison.

He was approaching forty but he felt even older today. Although fit for his age he wondered how he would shape up in the gym against Nicola's immaculate physique. At least in his personal gym there would be no male competition. On the way back from her flat she had implored him to work out with her. Her reasons had sounded rehearsed: firstly, that no one should work out alone, in case of accidents, and secondly that he might need to show her his equipment - said with a perfectly straight face. After his sombre thoughts at her flat he hadn't the heart to refuse, even though after last night's scene at the hotel he strongly suspected an ulterior motive. Well, he thought, he must simply discipline her all the more, to keep her brazen behaviour in check.

In truth James knew he was deeply attracted to Nicola. Nicola knew it, too. His yearning for her was like nothing he had felt for years. It made him angry with her, wanting to punish her all the more for it, yet he suspected it was that she craved. It seemed like a spiralling cycle of desire. He gave the orders, but he sometimes believed she had written the script. Their next scene was patently obvious, but what concerned him more was what the final curtain would bring, since one member of the cast had yet to appear on stage.

When he returned to the study Nicola told him she had decided to work through lunch, to make sure everything was finished before they went to the gym. James normally missed lunch anyway so he was happy with the arrangement.

Soon after two o'clock he could not wait any longer. He told Nicola to leave anything she had left until tomorrow. After the morning's early start she deserved to finish work early. He suspected she could guess the real reason for his impatience.

The gym was across the tiled entrance hall. It had its own adjoining changing room and shower. Beyond that was an indoor pool. Images of Nicola in a bikini, her glistening wet body bending over for him, he set aside for another day.

A small range of stainless steel weight machines were set out around the gym's mirrored walls. For aerobic workouts a jogger, an exercise bike and a rower stood by the windows, which looked out over the frosty winter parkland at the back of the house.

James changed first while Nicola looked around the machines. He was warming up on the exercise bike when she joined him in her kit. She did some stretching exercises on the mat nearby. She wore pink and white trainers, a pink cropped top and tight white lycra shorts. It seemed that most of the clothes in her wardrobe were designed to display her gorgeous bottom to advantage.

He finished on the bike and moved across to the lat pull down machine. While he exercised he watched her in a mirror. He didn't bother to disguise it; he knew she expected him to watch her.

Nicola chose the jogger and lightly pounded the treadmill, looking out at the garden and the low winter sun. From time to time he glanced at her athletic movements, and of course, her flexing buttocks. The gym had been cool at first, after the warm study, but after thirty minutes of steady work they'd both warmed up considerably.

She stopped the jogger and came to a standstill, leaning forward with hands on knees.

'Phew, feel better for that,' she panted. 'I need to do legs and abs today.' She looked around. 'Haven't you got a leg curl?'

He pointed to the machine in the corner.

'Oh, that's not like the one at my gym. On ours you sit on it and push your calves down to exercise the back of your thighs.'

He knew the type she meant. 'This is just as good,' he said. 'I'll show you.'

He demonstrated, lying face down over the bench, hooking his feet under the ankle pads and raising his calves to stretch his strong hamstrings. James still had a powerful build. Although not now as fit as in his youth he was still quite athletic in appearance. It was her turn to see something of the tautness of his gluts beneath his shorts and his well-defined leg muscles.

'You try.' He got off the machine, set the weight peg at a low level and shortened the length of the bar to the ankle pads. She lay facedown on the bench, gripping the handles at the front and putting her feet under the pads. He watched her as she slowly lifted her calves. The slightly inverted 'V' shape of the bench naturally raised her bottom, but she was lifting it even higher, off the bench, which was incorrect.

'Keep your hips down or you could hurt your back,' he told her. She tried again with the same result, so he put his hand on her bottom and pressed. Nicola continued, doing a set of twenty repetitions with James holding her down.

She stopped and he removed his hand, but she didn't get up. The material of her shorts was stretched as tightly as possible and semi see-through. By now it was a little damp with perspiration from her exertions. Through it he could make out her white G-string and some faint marks on her skin from her caning. There were a few beads of sweat in the hollow of her firm back. He looked at her hair, wet at the tips but glossy in spite of her workout.

She let go of the machine's handles and folded her arms on the bench. Resting the side of her head on them, she looked up at him invitingly with her hazel eyes. He knelt by the machine and rested his hand on her bottom again. She moved her buttocks gently under his touch and smiled at him.

'I take it you've decided that you want your beating in here today,' he said dryly.

'I'll have it wherever you'd like to give it me, sir, but now you've got me in a good position...' she replied, with her unique combination of meekness and cheek.

He stroked her leg with his fingertips, in no

hurry to begin. He felt like Keats' knight-at-arms in thrall to the faery's child. All his intentions of resisting her were slipping away.

Outside the sun was setting and the room was becoming dark and chilly. He got to his feet and switched on the lights. He pressed a button which closed the window blinds and another to turn the thermostat up. He looked at her from the wall.

'I'll fetch them,' he said. 'You look comfy; make sure you don't go to sleep.'

'I'm sure you'll wake me up soon enough if I do,' she said, smiling.

When James returned Nicola was lying in the same position waiting for him. He put down the cane and lotion and stood over her holding the strap. She roused herself, gripped the handles and looked at the floor in front of the machine.

'Are you ready, Nicola?'

'Yes, sir.'

He took up a suitable position to begin. Since she was lying more or less horizontally below him, with just a bend in the bench raising her bottom slightly, he decided to deliver the strokes vertically downwards. He raised the strap in his right hand until it fell over his right shoulder. He paused then brought it down with a hard crack on the target. She shuddered and counted the stroke.

'One, sir.'

'Just eleven more to go today, Nicola.'

'Thank you for reminding me, sir,' was her impertinent response.

He stood a little further back to allow himself a wider swing, and then planted a juicy second across the full width of her buttocks. It gave a loud and satisfying thwack.

'Ow! Two, sir,' she screeched.

As he delivered the third stroke he noticed her buttocks tense just before it landed and caught her glancing up to see in the mirror when the stroke would come. James had anticipated this would happen in the mirrored room, and had come prepared. He took a black leather eye mask from the pocket of his shorts and stooped to pull it over her eyes. She said nothing, but lay passively as he gently worked the elastic under her hair and over her ears.

James delivered a sharp fourth stroke to untensed buttocks, put down the strap and then said, 'Roll your shorts down.'

She moved her hands back to her waistband and eased them over her reddening behind, lifting it slightly from the bench. He put his hand under her pelvis to stop her lying down again. Supporting herself by her knees on the bench she moved her hands back to the handles, leaving her bottom raised in the air. It pleased him that she always understood so quickly what he wanted her to do.

James straightened the G-string, which had been dislodged as the shorts lowered. He pulled the rolled shorts a little further down to just above her knees, and found himself squeezing and slapping her bottom and then gently caressing it. Then he pushed his right hand between her thighs and under her string. He let his fingers brush over the silky hair there, tracing the small neat triangle. As he rubbed the pads of his fingers gently over it

Nicola sighed quietly in appreciation. He slipped his middle finger easily between her moist lips. He caressed her there for a few moments before withdrawing his hand.

'We must finish your punishment first,' he said.

'I know,' she replied quietly.

He pushed her down on the bench again and took up the strap. From this angle the base of her buttocks and the tops of her thighs were an easier target than her normal bending position. It was an area which had received too little attention on Monday, so with the final two strokes of the strap he intended to put right the omission. Her gentle sighs were replaced by yelps of pain as the two lashes hit home hard in and around the crease between cheeks and thighs. They were more brutal strokes than she'd had so far with the strap, and after each she raised her calves, almost completing a leg curl. Each time she held the weight in position for some seconds with thighs and buttocks tense, which seemed to help her bear the pain. Finally she would relax her legs and count the stroke.

'Now just the six strokes of the cane left,' he said.

She groaned. There was no clever rejoinder this time.

He helped her to stand and she gingerly pulled up her shorts and then stood, blindfolded, waiting for him to guide her. The gym was now warm and he took off his sweatshirt.

'Do you use the hyper extension?' he asked.

'Yes, sir. The machine at our gym is just like

yours here.'

'Good. That's where I'll cane you today. Take off your top.'

She obeyed, removing it carefully to avoid dislodging the eye mask. He led her by the hand across the gym to the piece of equipment in question, which stood facing the middle of the opposite wall.

From a heavy base a three inch square white metal arm came up at forty-five degrees to the floor. At the top of the arm was a large black pad to support the pelvis and the tops of the thighs, which he adjusted to her height. At the base were two roller pads to hold the ankles. He stood her feet by them either side of the bar. Then standing behind her he held her tightly for a moment. He gripped her breasts beneath his left forearm and pulled her back into him.

'Ooh, I like the hairy chest,' she whispered, rubbing her shoulder blades against him.

He placed his right hand over her stomach and forced her bottom against his shorts. He could feel her sway her buttocks to rub against his erect penis. Then he guided her down to rest on the pad. She was now leaning along the forty-five degree bar supported by the pads over her ankles and under her thighs.

'Arms folded across your chest. Now show me a few abs reps.'

In a controlled movement Nicola lowered her upper body towards the floor and raised it. Below the waist the bar held her body still; above she was working her lower back and abdominal muscles. On the downward movement her hair hung loose inches above the floor. After ten repetitions he told her to stop and remain upright.

He took up the cane and swished it in the air a few times. Nicola remained quite still, her arms crossed against her naked breasts. James played the cane over her shorts, tracing the full, round buttocks, deliberately extending the time she was being made to maintain her posture. Although standing slightly behind her he could see her front reflected in the mirrored wall. The masked eyes, the frown of concentration on her pretty face as she tried to maintain her position. He looked at the clear outline of her abdominal muscles gently moving with her breathing.

Acting on a vicious impulse he changed the cane to his left hand and brought his right hand down on her left buttock. Her body shook with the force of his blow.

'One, sir. Um... maybe not,' she said.

'You know that was a spank and not the cane, Nicola. You will now receive one extra cane stroke.'

'Yes, sir.'

He raised the cane again and brought it down very hard with a loud swish across the backs of her thighs. She cried out with pain and flung her hands down to her legs. He waited for twenty seconds while she rubbed them, and then said, 'One extra stroke for moving your hands out of position, one for not counting. You will have eight more strokes.'

'Oh no, I can't take that many!' she wailed.

'Would you like to end now?' he asked. 'My original offer for you to leave is still open. And I want to remind you now that the severity of the session will increase on Friday.'

Nicola sighed heavily. She folded her arms back in place and stiffened her position along the bar.

'I'm ready now, sir. Please continue with the caning.'

'Count from the beginning again. These will come quickly.'

He straightened the lycra over her bottom so it was completely smooth. Then he took up the cane and, without any pause, delivered three strokes immediately one after the other across her buttocks.

'One, sir! Two, sir! Three, sir!' she howled.

'Give me ten repetitions,' he demanded. 'You wanted an abdominal workout today.'

She dipped and raised her upper body ten times. 'My gluts are getting a good working over as well,' she murmured.

As she exercised he could see lines from the cane forming under her shorts. Perspiration from her back and the cleft of her bottom made the thin material even more transparent.

He rested the cane on her buttocks as her exercises stretched and relaxed them. When she had completed her set he told her to remain in the dipped position, and as she bent forward from the waist the support pad of the machine splayed her buttocks perfectly. 'Support yourself with your hands on the floor and keep still.' With her arms straight she was just able to rest her fingertips on the floor.

Four and five were severe strokes delivered to the broadened target. Then he rolled down her shorts, leaving them around her knees, and tore off the flimsy G-string.

For the next two strokes he started the cane from high behind his head. Each one cracked down, cutting into her naked bottom, raising a large weal and making her scream. After each stroke Nicola had to pause sobbing for a full minute before she was able to speak.

As she counted, 'Seven, sir,' he could hear the tears in her voice. He told her to adopt an upright position again, this time with hands on head. She complied, sobbing. Her back and stomach were wet with sweat. Her once smooth tanned bottom was dark red and raised with weals. Small, dark bruises were appearing on some of the cane marks.

'One stroke remaining.'

He set the cane in place across her buttocks again, giving firm taps with it on existing bruises. Then once again he was driven by an impulse to extend her suffering. He put down the cane, watching her wondering beneath her mask when the next stroke would come. He picked up the bottle of lotion and squeezed some directly onto her beaten cheeks. She gasped at its coolness, and then yelped as he began massaging it roughly into her bottom. He slapped it on her buttocks, gripping and squeezing them as he worked the lotion over their full round surface and the tops of her legs.

The glowing punished skin was hot to the touch. He pushed his right hand between her legs and gently inserted his forefinger between the lips of her vagina. It was hot and wet. He couldn't bear this any longer. His erection was stiff and throbbing. He was overcome with a desire to plunge it into her now. He pulled his shorts down and stepped out of them.

He pushed his penis between her legs. 'I can't wait any longer.' He was consumed by lust for her.

'Please sir, you must finish my strokes for today.' He could hear the arousal in her voice.

'I'll let you off the last one. In any case by Friday you'll be begging me to stop beating you,' he said cruelly.

'Please, sir, you must give me the last stroke for today,' Nicola pleaded with him. Tears were rolling down her cheeks from under the mask.

'Very well,' he said irritably. He picked up the cane and rested it across her backside. 'You asked for this,' he said angrily.

He took the cane all the way back and swung his body round, slashing it with all his might into her bottom. Nicola's body squirmed and jerked in agony. She flung her head back and let out a long, anguished howl. She managed to keep her balance but her hands shot down to hold the bar. James dropped the cane and gripped her arms from behind as she twisted her torso from side to side. He planted his legs either side of hers and would not let go of her until she stilled herself.

'Next time I'm going to give you an extra stroke

for that display. But no more now.' He kissed her damp hair and face as she tried to free herself. But she was pinned against the bar by his weight and held above the waist by his strong arms.

'Don't you want me now? Weren't all your tricks to make this happen?' he growled at her.

Later he couldn't believe how rough he had been. He had felt nothing but animal aggression and lust. There was a madness in his brain that could be satisfied by sex with her alone. His penis was jammed upright against her right buttock. He was thrusting his pelvis into her, squashing her against the pad of the machine as hard as he could.

He gripped her hair and slowly pulled her head back and down so he could look into her face.

'Well?' he rasped into her ear.

'Yes, I want you,' she cried back.

He pulled her off the equipment and she stumbled, with the shorts still around her knees. He grabbed her to stop her from falling and pushed her up against the mirror on the wall. She was panting and perspiring. She shook one leg out from the shorts as they fell to the floor. Supporting herself against the mirror with the palms of her hands she stuck out her backside with her legs wide apart, inviting him in. With a hand gripping each buttock he pulled them apart to open wide the lips of her pink vagina while he pushed his penis in. For both of them the relief was palpable, to be joined at last, after days of her seductive foreplay.

He felt her heat envelope his penis. Gripping the fronts of her thighs he thrust rhythmically in and out. While he grunted with pleasure she moaned. When he was nearing orgasm he withdrew, wanting to draw out the bliss as long as he could. He took the bottle of lotion and spread some over her bottom. When it glowed with a scarlet sheen he stood back and began to smack each cheek. With each blow she yelped. Then he entered her again, pumping vigorously.

'I'm ready, come now,' she implored him.

But he didn't. Holding himself back he withdrew again and rained short slaps over the cane marks on her buttocks and legs.

When her whimpering was loud enough to satisfy him he stopped and thrust his pulsing erection into her again, gripping her hips to draw her onto him. Their perspiration mingled with the lotion on her buttocks to lubricate their bodies. Then he pushed her flat up against the glass. With his knees slightly bent and thrusting up into her, pressing her against the glass, squeezing her buttocks with his hands, finally he came. She shrieked in pain or enjoyment he could not tell. He held her pressed against the glass, both breathing heavily, biting her neck and shoulders. She had begun to cry again and seemed ready to collapse when he released her.

Panting heavily he lifted her sagging body in his arms and carried her to the exercise mat. He laid her down, rolling her onto her front and lay down beside her. From time to time he stroked and kissed her back, her neck, the side of her face and the warm, bruised cheeks of her bottom.

They lay like that for some time, and he was

beginning to feel he was ready to make love to her again when she said she'd better go.

He lay on the mat thinking, while she showered and dressed. When she came out of the changing room he rose and kissed her. They held their embrace for a while. She sighed contentedly and swayed a little in his arms. 'James, I'm glad we did this before...' she paused.

'Before Rebecca returns?' he finished, and she nodded.

Eventually he released her and said with mock severity, 'Well don't think this will make me go easy on you on Friday.'

'Of course not,' she agreed.

At the door she stopped and grinned at him. She put her hands on her bottom, now back in the tight black pants, and mouthed, 'Ouch.'

After she had gone he looked forward impatiently to Friday. It would be the last session and he wondered how to make it special. He half expected that Nicola would propose something herself. After all, she had come up with the idea of the gym.

Chapter 7

After the evening in the gym James had expected awkwardness between them at work, but any tension seemed to be on his side. Nicola was early again on Thursday, cheerful and full of life. If only he could relax it would have been a pleasure to be around her. Apart from the occasional accidental contact she avoided enticing him, and he was relieved that she kept to her own office for most of the day.

That afternoon James had something important to do. After consulting a number of reference works he decided to his own satisfaction that the painting he'd seen in London was a forgery. There had been one or two unsavoury rumours about Francesco's Gallery in the past, and James thought the best course of action would be to go straight to the police. With a more reputable gallery he would have spoken to the owners first, but he had a niggling suspicion that Francesco himself could be involved. A conference call with the Art and Antiques Squad at New Scotland Yard lasted over an hour.

Soon after he put the phone down Nicola came in to say goodbye for the evening. Shyly she pecked him on the cheek, and as she turned to leave he made an impulsive offer.

'Nick.'

She stopped and turned back expectantly.

'After the final session tomorrow, would you like to spend the night here?' he asked quietly.

In case he was sounding too soft, he added, 'You might be in too much pain to drive home.'

She smiled and said she would like that very much indeed. So that was that. Now all he had to do was pass a restless night in impatient expectation of the morrow. He did not have to meet Rebecca at the airport until Saturday evening, so there would be plenty of time to erase the traces of Nicola's stay.

Friday morning passed without incident, but with James less and less able to concentrate on his work. Nicola had brought her overnight bag, so it was clear that she still intended to stay. Shortly after lunch she spoke to him on the intercom from her office.

'Since today is to be my last punishment, sir,' she said, 'I wanted to wear something special.' Her use of 'sir' told him she was in her role of obedience. He said nothing.

'I need you to approve it, sir. If you're not satisfied I'll go home and fetch whatever clothes you wish.'

'Very well,' he said with affected sternness. 'Let me see.'

Nicola appeared at the study door dressed head to toe in red lingerie. When he met her eyes he saw them brighten with pleasure at his appreciative gasp. His gaze travelled down the satin corset, to the red lace briefs and sheer stockings. She wore perilously high heels, also in red. In her hair were two tiny red horns and she held a toy pitchfork. She walked to the middle of the floor and twirled for him. The strings of the corset were drawn so tightly that he was puzzled how she could have done it herself, until he saw the discreet fasteners at the front.

'You said I was a devil, sir.' She pouted glossy red lips.

He pushed his chair back from his desk and told her to come to him. She obeyed, smiling, and stood between him and the desk. She handed the plastic pitchfork to him, turned and put her hands on the desk, leaning over to thrust her bottom provocatively towards him. He reached out to touch the silk ribbon suspenders and the stocking seams, which she had ensured were perfectly straight. His hand followed the contours of her shapely cheeks through the transparent gauze of the briefs.

Trying to retain the upper hand against yet another seductive onslaught, he said, 'This is not just a game, young lady; you must learn your lesson.'

That was something he needed to tell himself, he thought. He had gone far beyond the bounds of eccentric office discipline. In reality he was having an affair with Nicola, whilst engaged to Rebecca.

'Yes, sir,' she pouted, not seeming to mind his harsh words. She swayed from side to side enticingly. He slapped her leg with the pitchfork.

'Keep still,' he ordered. He went on tapping her behind with the thin plastic rod, gradually making the blows harder.

She did not object. She knew she'd had the desired effect, he thought. What could he do to regain the initiative? Make a new rule, of course.

'You may wear this for today's session. However, the clothes in which you are disciplined must be worn in the office during the day. Therefore you must stay dressed as you are all afternoon.'

Then, knowing he was condemning himself to

an afternoon of agony, he added, 'And by the way, I'll need you in here to take dictation.'

'Yes sir, of course. I'll just get my pad.'

When Nicola returned he moved over to the Chesterfield sofa, where they would be more comfortable. He took across some papers relevant to the letters and put them on the coffee table.

Nicola sat serenely at his side taking down his words, as if fully dressed. As he spoke he surreptitiously glanced at her lingerie. He could tell it was of high quality. Later, he thought, he would get a chance to look at the label.

They worked for an hour, and then he decided to have a break. He asked her to pour him a scotch. James rarely drank during the day, but this was not an ordinary day. He watched her walk to the drinks cabinet, her slender stockinged legs moving gracefully, even in the four inch heels. She returned with the drink.

'May I sit on your knee?'

He parted his legs to make room for her. Why fight it? he thought.

'Are you warm enough?' he asked.

'I am now,' she replied, drawing closer to his body.

He sipped his drink in silence for a while, conscious of her weight in his lap; his erection against her leg; her fresh scent; and the soft young skin of her arm resting around his neck.

'You remind me so much of Edward,' she said at last.

James was not sure he was pleased to hear this. Edward had been twenty years his senior. She must have guessed his thoughts.

'I don't mean in age,' she said quickly, 'although of course, you are both figures of authority for me. Really I mean that you have his kindness and good manners.'

'Well, I suppose we had similar backgrounds.'

'I loved him as much as I loved my father. More, I suppose, because as I grew older I learned to love him in a grown up way. I never had that chance with my father.'

He told her that Edward had been his tutor at university. 'Afterwards he was always a good friend.'

'When I was eighteen I did something very wrong that could have soured our relationship,' she said softly.

He noticed she blushed at the memory, and waited for her to continue.

'But I was fortunate. It didn't because he wouldn't let it. In fact, he used it to do something he'd promised my mother he would do: something that strengthened our love, but which was rather unconventional.'

She had already told him the punch line on Monday. 'He caned you,' he said.

'Yes, and much harder than you did!' she laughed, then without going into too much detail she told him about how she 'confessed' six times a year.

'It went on for three years. I think he'd been hoping to stop sooner, once I found a compatible lover. But I never did. Finally he thought I wasn't looking hard enough, so he stopped them when I was twenty-one.'

'Why twenty-one?' James asked out of curiosity.

'They had to stop sometime. That age was the start of true adulthood for people of Edward's generation. It seemed sensible at the time. Of course he became ill soon after, so they wouldn't have gone on much longer anyway.'

Something odd that she'd said came back to him. 'Why did your mother want him to beat you?' he asked.

'Well I didn't know that until I was twenty-one, when Edward told me the full story. He'd had an affair with my mother lasting many years. She was sexually submissive and my father simply didn't get it.'

'Did he know about your mother's affair with Edward?'

'Yes, he encouraged it. Edward believed him to have affairs of his own, so it was sauce for the goose, really.'

'Why didn't your parents divorce?'

'In spite of their sexual differences they loved each other. And there was me to think about. Edward said he asked her to marry him many times, but she would never consider it. He wasn't really sure that she didn't love my father more than she loved him. In the end, I suppose, caring for me was a sort of consolation prize for him.'

The afternoon light had begun to fade and the study was in shadows. James' drink was untouched on the table. It was an enlightening story in many ways. For one thing, here was the reason that his old friend had never married.

'I'm surprised your father agreed to Edward adopting you in their will,' he said, eager for her to continue.

'Edward said that the two of them got on fine. As you would expect they couldn't really be friends, but they respected one another. I suppose for both my parents to die seemed so unlikely that my father didn't really worry. And my mother insisted.'

'Why?'

'Well, to answer your earlier question, she could trust Edward - and only Edward - to force me to explore my sexuality without taking advantage of me.'

James nodded. He knew Edward to be a man of honour.

'If my nature turned out to be submissive, she wanted me to have the chance of fulfilment that she'd found with him. They agreed that the beatings wouldn't start until I was an adult. Then I would be old enough to make informed choices about the sensations I uncovered. With his experience, Edward would be able to tell straight away whether or not I needed discipline.'

'But wasn't it traumatic for you when your guardian of more than a decade suddenly wanted to spank you?' James asked, unable to imagine how Edward could have carried it off.

'Unwittingly I gave him the perfect opportunity by doing something seriously wrong. After that it was easy for him; if I hadn't responded he would have backed off from further beatings. He could claim that one time had been justified and our relationship wouldn't have been too damaged.

'But Edward was a clever man. Even before he first put me over his knee I think he knew I was submissive.'

'How?'

'Well don't forget he was experienced, like you. And more importantly he'd spotted the clues over the years. Remember those old westerns where the hero has to spank the heroine before they get together? When I was a little girl I was glued to those scenes.'

'I remember them,' he laughed. 'I enjoyed them too.'

'Once when I was a teenager he caught me watching a video of *Belle de Jour*. He came in just as Catherine Deneuve was about to be whipped. I moved my hand from my pants pretty quickly, but I think he saw it.'

The room was growing cold and James was conscious that the girl was half naked. He turned up the heating, switched on some gentle lighting and drew the curtains. Sitting beside her again he pulled her to him and kissed her. The revelations had made him feel much closer to her. He unclipped the top two hooks of the corset and slipped his hands under the satin, to fondle her breasts. She held him round the neck and kissed him again.

'James, I have a confession to make,' she said timidly. 'Two, actually.'

'The place for confessions is across my lap,' he told her, reverting to his stern voice. 'Then I can react appropriately.'

Compliantly she pulled herself across his lap before she continued.

'I would understand if you wanted to sack me, but I need to be honest with you. I've grown so fond of you.'

'What is it?' He was intrigued.

'I told you that I'd seen you caning Rebecca a few weeks ago.'

He remembered she'd said as much on Monday. 'Yes.' As he listened his fingers traced the flowery pattern in the lace of the panties.

'At first it was an accident, but I didn't just see it and go; I stayed to watch for ages.'

'I see,' he said, although it didn't really worry him. His hand moved under the lace panties and he pinched her buttocks. There were noticeable bruises remaining from Wednesday. Today's beating would be particularly painful over the still tender spots.

'You were so severe with her.' Nicola sounded impressed.

'Well Rebecca should have known better.' James felt no need to justify his fiancée's harsh treatment.

'I was excited and I decided to try to make you do it to me.' She spoke more slowly now. James thought they were coming to the important admission.

'Go on,' he told her. By now his hand had moved on to stroke her inner thighs. Nicola opened her legs slightly to let him.

'So I deliberately held up that buy order you gave me,' she said.

'Are you saying you lost me that money on purpose?' he asked crossly. His hand stopped its explorations and rested on her right buttock.

She sounded scared. 'I didn't know it would cost you that much. I just wanted you to find me out and punish me.'

James thought furiously about the wasted money. An honest mistake was easily forgivable, but this scheming was much less so. Agitated by his silence Nicola tried to turn round to look at him, but he held her down.

'I can't tell you how sorry I was when you were about to sack me,' she explained anxiously. 'I realised I'd gone too far and I was about to lose everything.'

'I hope the feeling taught you not to scheme like that again.'

'Oh it did,' she reassured him.

'And the beating I'm going to inflict on you tonight will reinforce the lesson.'

Now she knew he was not going to fire her, her body relaxed across his lap.

'Yes, sir. Thank you, sir,' she said meekly.

'What you did was very wrong, but you have owned up to it when you didn't have to,' he told her. 'If you'd said nothing I would never have known. Nevertheless...' he felt her stiffen again as he paused, '...six of the strap and six of the cane are not a sufficient sentence. I need to think carefully about what you are to receive, but I can assure you it will be much more than we had planned.'

'I deserve whatever you choose to do to me, sir.'

'To begin with it will be a good spanking,' he said, suiting his actions to the words. He continued to slap her bottom heavily for some minutes, then he took down her panties and continued. After a while he felt her slip her hand between her legs. Roughly he grasped her wrists in his left hand and held them in the small of her back.

'If I am waiting until tonight, so will you,' he said.

After a good ten minutes of this treatment Nicola began to writhe in the pain of each blow. James' hand was itself stinging and he paused for a moment, letting it recover, resting on the warmth of her burning cheeks. Her bottom was a deep rosy flush, but he didn't feel inclined to let her off just yet. Instead he told her to fetch the plastic pitchfork. She held it out to him and stood spellbound as he gripped the trident end and tested it against his hand. After his angry response to her confession her eyes were bright with a new excitement.

The plastic rod was not as punishing as the cane of course, but it would do for now. He stood up. 'Hold out your right hand,' he commanded.

Nicola's eyes widened with astonishment, but she obeyed.

He snapped the rod across her palm. She winced and curled up her hand. He repeated the stroke twice, before demanding her left hand. Her eyes were filled with tears. As she watched the rod fall she cringed, but she had the courage to keep her hand still, which he praised.

'Good girl,' he said encouragingly, after the last stroke. 'Stand up straight.'

He inspected her appearance carefully, noting how her wriggles and their embraces had disarranged her underwear.

'I'll give you ten minutes to freshen up. Then I want to see you back in here.'

While Nicola was away James poured himself another drink and thought about the story she had related.

When she returned she looked as good as new. She had brushed her hair, washed her face and refreshed her gloss lipstick. He told her to turn round, and noted that the crooked seams of her stockings had been carefully straightened.

'Are you ready for the next stage of your punishment?'

'Yes, sir,' came her prompt response.

'Now, was this the chair,' he asked, his hand on one of the low leather armchairs, 'over which you saw Rebecca caned?'

Nicola nodded.

'Then you know what to do.'

She approached the chair and bent over it, resting her hands on the seat cushion. The back of the chair fitted snugly into her hips, spreading her bottom. James made sure her legs were together, his hand lingering on the lovely flesh exposed above the stocking tops. He smoothed her panties across her bottom.

'I've considered your errant behaviour, miss, and I've decided to double the number of strokes of the strap you are to receive.'

James paused but she said nothing; she must know there is more to come, he thought.

'And to triple the number with the cane. You will have twelve strokes of the strap and eighteen of the cane.'

'Yes, sir. Thank you, sir.' She spoke firmly, clearly expecting something along these lines.

'As I beat you I shall bear in mind your comment about the hardness of Edward's delivery. Afterwards I hope you will be able to compare me more favourably to him.'

'Yes, sir.'

'As an overture we shall begin with twelve strokes with this rod.'

Nicola squealed and flinched as the implement tore into her twelve times. Light though it was, it left distinct dark stripes across a behind still pink from its spanking.

At the end he told her to fetch the strap and cane from the cupboard, and set them at the end of the oak coffee table. He had her bring a cushion from her office, and then ordered her to kneel on all fours on the table, with the cushion protecting her knees. He adjusted her position.

'Feet together,' he commanded, 'back, arms and upper legs all straight.'

She was made to face the implements he was to use.

'I want you to look at them,' he said with a cruel smile, 'and imagine them cutting into your beautiful backside in one hour's time.

He sat on the sofa with his drink, working at some papers. From time to time he would look up to check she was keeping a good posture, and to admire her chastised buttocks. Mentally he made a note to tackle some of the soft flesh of her upper legs, which so far today had been left untouched.

But as the evening turned out James' plans came to nothing. Shortly before six o'clock, when Nicola had been kneeling on the table for about thirty minutes, they heard the sound of a car coming to a halt on the gravel drive. Nicola had been starting to get fidgety and she used the sound as an excuse to ease back onto her haunches. James went to the window and looked out from behind the curtains.

'It's Rebecca, in a taxi!' he said, shocked and immediately flustered. There was a dismayed squeak and a rush of air behind him as Nicola shot out of the room like a startled rabbit. James quickly put away the implements and tidied the room, and just had time to open the window to waft away some of Nicola's scent, when the key turned in the front door and Rebecca called out to him.

James welcomed her with as much affection as he could muster, the same arms having held Nicola so little time before. His genuine surprise at her arrival helped to cover what she might otherwise have taken as reticence on his part. Rebecca explained that she had decided to come home a day early.

'Were you not enjoying the skiing?'

'Of course, but I missed you,' she said, slumping down on the Chesterfield sofa. 'And it gives me an extra day to prepare for work on Monday.'

Surreptitiously James sniffed to see if Nicola's scent still hung about this corner of the study. Rebecca had a very sensitive nose, and when she heard a bump from the girl's office her head shot round.

'Is Nicola still here?' She sounded surprised; Nicola normally left at four on a Friday.

'Yes. There was something she needed to finish.'

Rebecca rose and went into the outer office to say hello. James followed, for no very good reason, he realised.

Nicola was just zipping up her overnight bag. She was still flushed from her afternoon exertions and trying to hide it by appearing to be in a rush. They exchanged brief greetings.

'Are you going away for the weekend?' enquired Rebecca.

Nicola replied in the affirmative. James was worried that Rebecca had noticed her glossy lipstick, which seemed an odd choice for a day at the office. At least James had had the presence of mind to wipe his face and lips.

'Well you better get going, Nicola. I'm sure James doesn't want work to eat into any more of your personal time.'

That night they sat in silence in the living room, sharing a bottle of wine. James had showered, saying he needed to change after a tiring day, and hoping that any trace of Nicola would be removed. Rebecca had showered too, to freshen herself after the journey. Before they dressed they made love. It was fortunate he'd not had sex with

Nicola, so he could easily play the hungry lover who had been celibate for ten days. But when he closed his eyes he saw Nicola, a vision in red stockings.

Mixing business with pleasure had always been anathema for James. He was concerned that it would be impossible for him to work properly if Nicola continued as his secretary. He would seek reasons to punish her again. In fact, he knew she would find ways to make sure he did. It just wouldn't be a workable office set up. Yet he didn't want to lose her.

If Nicola were not his secretary he was forced to ask himself the difficult question: precisely what role did he see her playing in his life? James had believed he'd always been honest and honourable. His first marriage ended in an amicable divorce some years before, but the cause had not been the infidelity of either party. It was not in his nature to retain a mistress, and he knew his first love was Rebecca. Nicola drove him to distraction with desire, and he had become passionately fond of her, but they would not be compatible as life partners.

Furthermore, although Nicola was prepared to flirt and sleep with an older man she was unlikely to wish to marry one. She was still rather young to be married at all, he thought, knowing that many would consider him a stick-in-the-mud for such a view. Edward had often reminded him that a typical age for a girl to be married in Renaissance Italy was thirteen. He, in turn, reminded Edward that life expectancy in the fifteenth century was thirty or less; if they hadn't married young they may not have had time to raise a family.

'Shall we eat out tonight? It would be a nice end to my holiday.' Rebecca's suggestion broke into his thoughts, and he found her looking at him curiously.

Recovering from his reverie he agreed at once and rose to phone a local restaurant. He realised that he should have been much more careful not to appear preoccupied. Not having seen Rebecca for over a week, she would expect him to be far more attentive.

He apologised. 'I'm sorry if I seem a bit woolly tonight. Francesco's called me to look at a painting. That's why I was in London. I think it's a forgery and I've spoken to the police.'

It was a good cover story because Rebecca was at once fascinated. 'You must tell me all about it over dinner.'

'I shall. After I've heard all about your holiday. And I think we'll take a taxi so we can toast your return with some champagne.'

Rebecca looked pleased as they left, and James thought he had managed to head off any suspicion.

The next morning a crate arrived at James' house, marked for the attention of Carlo Mancuso. Rebecca now had some explaining of her own to do. James learnt about the brilliant Carlo and how she wanted him to display his work exclusively through her firm.

'I see, but why has it been sent here?' he asked,

puzzled. 'Why didn't you have his work sent to your gallery?'

He could see that Rebecca was itching to tell him something. 'Because this one's not for public display,' she said, excitedly. 'Damn! I wish I hadn't promised Carlo not to open it. He said he had some finishing touches to make, but it looked finished to me.'

She made up her mind. 'I'm going to open it anyway,' she said firmly.

'Even though you promised not to?' James was only mildly surprised, knowing well enough the duplicity of women in minor matters.

'Well it's my painting!' she insisted.

'Oh, well that's fine then,' he replied, to placate her. He felt he was getting better at keeping Rebecca's temper on an even keel. He asked whether she meant she had bought it or that it was a portrait of her.

'Both,' she replied. She smiled enigmatically and asked him to go to his study for a while.

After half an hour or so James heard her calling him. He returned to the living room, but all that was there were an open wooden crate and some torn packaging. Her voice came from upstairs and he went up to find her naked on his bed.

'Do you think it's a good likeness?' she purred.

The painting was propped on an armchair. He was instantly mesmerised by its quality and, of course, its subject.

'Carlo does a good line in Velázquez,' he marvelled.

Rebecca was elated with the effect the painting

had on him. She jumped up like an excited schoolgirl and clung to his arm as they admired it together.

'What to you think of his line in Rebeccas?' she asked playfully.

Realising that Rebecca meant this as a gift for him, James was careful to be exceptionally complimentary. And it was not difficult, because he truly did love the work.

'You're more beautiful than the original Venus,' he said, clasping her to him.

'Have you noticed the pinkness of her cheeks?' she asked innocently, unbuttoning his shirt...

Later they lay on the bed sipping champagne.

'There's no question where this is going to hang,' he said, indicating the wall in front of his bed.

'I think I'll have it reframed first,' she said. 'Carlo's chosen a very ugly one.'

James had to agree. He got off the bed to examine it. 'It's very heavy, too,' he said. He studied the painting once again, more carefully.

'Did you say Carlo's come back with you?' he asked absently. 'Have you left him at the cottage? I suppose we should have him over for dinner.'

'I've given him a luxury weekend in London. A couple of people from the gallery are showing him the sights. He'll come to the cottage on Monday.'

'You really are pulling out all the stops for him.'

'Don't you think he's worth it?'

'I'm sure he is, if this is a sample of his work.'

James began to peer at one part of the painting more closely, and Rebecca asked him what was wrong.

'It doesn't seem to have been mounted properly. Look.'

He laid it on the bed and pointed towards a tiny crease in the top right corner of the canvas. The area was darkly shaded, so the blemish was not easy to spot.

'It looks as though something has pushed it out of shape after it was mounted,' she said.

They looked at each other wide-eyed with the same surmise. A painting that appeared too heavy, a frame thicker than it needed to be and a stretch in the canvas; it all suggested that something was hidden behind her painting, and it didn't take either of them long to want to investigate.

James fetched a sharp knife and carefully cut away the masking tape and backboard. A faded Madonna on wood lay behind it, held in place by four supports connected to the thick frame. One of these had broken in transit, allowing the Madonna to rest against the canvas of Rebecca's portrait.

'I caught a glance of it in a cupboard in Carlo's studio,' she gasped. 'When I asked about it he was very coy.'

'And it is surprisingly similar to the forgery at Francesco's. It looks to me as if Carlo is responsible for both paintings.'

'We mustn't jump to conclusions. There could be an innocent explanation.'

'You mean you would rather not have your protégé arrested just yet,' he said dryly.

They mused in silence for a while.

'Coming so soon after the other affair, I'm

inclined to go to the police,' said James.

Rebecca pouted. 'Couldn't we just put it back and see what happens?'

'Surely you won't want to sign Carlo now?' he said.

Rebecca said nothing, and once more he found himself frowning at the business ethics of his future wife. Carlo might go to jail for forgery, but the publicity would create more interest in his original works. So long as her gallery did not handle any forgeries they could benefit without risking their reputation.

Seeing his disapproval, Rebecca coloured defensively.

'Even Michelangelo made copies of Roman statues and passed them off as originals,' she protested.

In the end he indulged her. They would replace the forgery and see what happened. Tomorrow was Sunday, so Rebecca could slip into work unnoticed and seal the frame up professionally before Carlo arrived. Before she did so, however, James took a small precaution.

Chapter 8

When Rebecca had spoken to Nicola on the phone from Italy she told her about Carlo, and how she was hoping to persuade the talented young artist to show his work with her gallery. Carlo would be brought over to be wined and dined, and Rebecca needed a pretty young date for him to take to the gallery's Christmas ball. Since, at that moment, Nicola had been eyeing the slowly fading erection of Rebecca's fiancé, she hadn't felt able to refuse. Yet she had not been looking forward to the added complexity of meeting Carlo while there was unfinished business with James. For one thing, if Carlo was as hot as Rebecca had said, and Nicola felt like sleeping with him, there would be the marks of James' cane on her bottom to explain. Back in England Rebecca called again to suggest that Nicola come over for drinks on Saturday. That way she and Carlo could break the ice and they would be more relaxed together at the ball, the following Friday.

All of which was why, ten days later, Nicola was sitting in her car outside Rebecca's cottage, reluctant to get out and knock on the door. It had been a sunny afternoon, but the light was already fading, giving the bare trees a sombre feel. Rebecca's place was set in a quarter acre of its own, a hundred yards or so from the village green; all thatched roof and old grey stone. Rebecca opened the door and ushered her into an oak-beamed living room. Lamps were on and the curtains already drawn.

Little concession had been made to Christmas decorations; apart from a host of festive cards arranged on strings along one wall, there was only a small tinsel tree covered with a few baubles.

Even at the best of times Nicola found the older woman a little intimidating, with her executive wardrobe and her short fuse, and today her greeting had been polite but ominously cool. It didn't help that the sight of Rebecca made Nicola feel guilty about James. All in all, this little soiree was not looking promising.

'Uomo from the Duomo' had been out sketching the English countryside and was now upstairs finishing off. Apparently an artist at work couldn't be interrupted, even if his absence seemed rather rude when Nicola had driven thirty miles to meet him.

'He'll be down soon,' said Rebecca. 'Let's have some wine while we wait.'

Naturally Nicola asked about the holiday, and received a rundown of the international talent available on the pistes and in the bars of Bergamo. It all sounded a little outside Nicola's league and she wondered if it were meant to. In return Rebecca asked about the recent trip to London, and whether James had given her enough time off work to see a show. This enquiry was made with such polite nonchalance that Nicola almost giggled, knowing full well the question Rebecca really wanted answered. Fortunately she bit her lip and talked in a matter of fact way about how much she had enjoyed her first visit to the National Gallery.

'Yes, James can be charming when he talks about art,' murmured Rebecca, refilling their glasses. It was a signal that the conversation was moving into deeper waters, because she continued, 'I wanted to ask you what you thought about James' other passion.'

'I don't understand?' Nicola's expression was one

of innocent enquiry; she could be nonchalant too.

There was a long pause; one that Nicola thought might be described as pregnant. It was certainly about to spawn a surprise for her.

'You were watching us that night,' said Rebecca.

'What?' gasped Nicola. 'When do you mean?'

'Don't pretend you don't remember. The study door wasn't quite closed and I saw you. You were supposed to have gone home.'

There was no point in pretending and Nicola came clean. 'I... I'd forgotten my gloves.'

'Well it took you long enough to get them; you were glued to the spot for half an hour.'

Watching the cane repeatedly whack across Rebecca's shapely backside, pressed over a leather armchair, had gripped Nicola, and she'd not been able to tear herself away. She admired the way Rebecca could take such severe chastisement with no more than squeals and squirms. Whilst James had limited Nicola's caning to six, Rebecca had not been so lucky. Welt after welt had appeared, and the white skin had turned deep red by the time he laid down the cane. And all for charging some clothes to his Amex.

Afterwards Rebecca had remained meekly in position while he took off his trousers and forced himself against her bruised buttocks. Seeing the tempestuous Rebecca tamed in this way had awed Nicola, and her hands shook as she picked up her gloves to leave. But she still couldn't understand how Rebecca had seen her when she had her back to her. Nicola blushed, ashamed at having stayed to watch the intimate scene and at having been found out.

'I'm sorry,' she said simply.

'Don't be,' said Rebecca. 'I didn't mind. Did I set a good example in how to take one's medicine?'

'Absolutely. I couldn't believe how brave you were.' Nicola was so obviously sincere and admiring that Rebecca smiled; it was the first sign of warmth she had shown. But her next words were not so warm.

'Were you as brave when he caned you?' she asked sharply, before Nicola realised where the questions were leading.

'He didn't... we didn't...' she stammered, starting to deny it, but her red face gave the game away again. She really must learn to lie better.

'Was the sex good, too?' That polite detachment again.

Nicola stared unhappily at the carpet and said nothing. In three cool questions Rebecca had confirmed everything. No wonder she held such a senior job, aged only thirty. Nicola's eyes began to fill up.

'Save the tears for later,' said Rebecca, unmoved. 'They may work better on Carlo.'

At that moment the door opened and the Italian entered.

'Has she confessed?' he asked, in deep, accented English.

'As good as,' replied Rebecca. 'Nicola, since you witnessed my punishment I think it's time for me to return the favour.'

Nicola knew by now what was to follow. She had come here with foreboding, but she'd failed to spot the real trap. In spite of her predicament she watched the newcomer intently. He seemed to be rearranging some of the furniture. Rebecca had been right about his looks; but there was something more, a feral magnetism. Although slightly built he lifted a heavy piano stool with ease, and smoothly placed it next to a small dining table Nicola had not noticed before. At some point the cottage's tiny living and dining rooms had evidently been knocked into this moderately sized room. When he disappeared again her eyes remained on the door through which he had passed. Fascination had overcome her rightful indignation that her Friday night date had still not spoken to her.

Rebecca was droning on, blaming Nicola for making James cheat on her. Nicola wanted to reply that James was an intelligent, grown man; he should be able to stop himself cheating if he wanted to. But she couldn't because she knew in her heart that she had been responsible; she suggested the caning when James wanted to sack her; she seduced him in the gym. James may have been complicit, but she had driven it along. Contrite, she admitted to herself that she probably deserved what was coming.

Carlo re-entered carrying two implements. It was plain enough what they were and for whom they were intended. Rebecca stood up and asked her to do the same. To make sure that Carlo saw her lovely figure, Nicola had dressed in tight faded blue jeans and a clinging black sweater. Rebecca made to take off the sweater and Nicola raised her arms to let her. Carlo stood still to watch and Nicola watched him back. She was beginning to feel like a rabbit down the barrels of his dark eyes. She shook her head to straighten her hair where the jumper had rumpled it. Then the three moved together to the table. Nicola was glad they let her keep her black bra on; she knew it made her cleavage look deep and shadowy. Not that Carlo would see much of it when it was pressed against the tabletop.

The wooden paddle lay ready on the table; an instrument of torture with which Nicola's bottom was so far unfamiliar. She knew it was favoured in American schools, cheerleaders being the victims of choice, and it added to the international flavour of the evening.

Carlo made her kneel on the piano stool and lean over the table. He pushed a cushion between her hips and the table edge to lift and spread her bottom. Rebecca faced her on the other side of the table, taking her hands and making her grip the far edge.

'Hold tight. Carlo can be merciless if you move out of position.'

Nicola wondered vaguely how Rebecca could know that. Even so, she did not miss the grim satisfaction in the words. 'How many strokes?' she asked meekly.

'It's better not to ask,' replied Rebecca.

There was a delay in which Nicola could hear her heart thudding. Perhaps Carlo was admiring her jean-clad behind. She hoped so, although it didn't bring her much comfort. Suddenly it began and he was laying into her with the paddle, pounding each cheek in turn until Nicola's eyes were squeezed shut with the pain. The cushion prevented her moving her bottom forward as the blows fell. Even though she gripped the table Rebecca held her wrists down strongly, so she couldn't move much even if she tried.

The strokes were no taps. Carlo was swinging his arm from high. After about a dozen blows he stopped and ran both his hands over her bottom. By now he would be able to feel its warmth through the denim, she thought. He patted and smacked it a few times, then she felt his hands move to the fastener and he tugged her jeans down. Nicola was wearing white shorts to avoid a panty line with the jeans.

'Boy shorts, Nicola?' laughed Rebecca. 'An extra layer. That's cheating.'

'No matter,' said Carlo. 'We begin again.'

He smoothed out the briefs where the jeans had shifted them, then resumed the paddling. So far Nicola had made no sounds other than heavier breathing, but now the stinging blows began to get to her and she gasped with each blow. Not knowing how many strokes she would receive made it much harder to bear.

Rebecca might have guessed what she felt, because she rubbed it home. 'There's still a long, long way to go, Nicola.'

Carlo stopped again to warm his hands on the soft cotton of her briefs. Being Italian he pinched her bottom until she yelped. Then he continued, bringing the flat of the wide wooden bat down across both cheeks. It seemed to be much worse than being paddled over the denim. At last he stopped. He took down her briefs and kneaded her naked buttocks for a minute or so. Any rest was welcome to her and she breathed more easily. At least the faint marks remaining from the severe gym caning would by now be hidden in an angry flush.

'And now we begin again,' he said, but Nicola had guessed that would happen. So the paddle smacked against her unprotected bottom and the blows cracked even louder than before. She just hoped twelve on her bare bum would be the end of it; he seemed to be grouping the spanking in dozens. She screwed up her face but she could feel tears run down her cheeks and drop on the polished oak table. Between her squeals she choked out an apology to Rebecca for wetting her table.

Rebecca seemed touched by this. She released Nicola's wrists and leaned forward to cradle the girl's head, stroking her hair. She whispered in her ear. 'There won't be much more of this. Then you can rest a while before the whipping.' Nicola groaned to hear confirmed what she knew earlier, when she saw the leather flogger.

No matter what Rebecca said it seemed Carlo didn't think the paddling was over yet. He was fiddling with her clothes once more. He had taken off her shoes and was now removing her jeans and briefs completely. She shifted her legs to help him. Then he tapped the inside of her legs with the paddle, indicating that he wanted her to spread her knees wide to the edges of the stool.

'I want your cheeks apart,' he told her.

So far her knees and thighs had been together, a pose which made her bum look its peachy best; or at least so she thought whenever she examined it in a mirror. But much more of her was on display now as Carlo confirmed by brushing his fingers over her pubic hair and the lips of her vagina, and in spite of her suffering Nicola was immediately aroused.

Carlo picked up the paddle once more and directed heavy blows relentlessly at her right bottom cheek. It was excruciating and she whimpered continuously. Rebecca held Nicola's head firmly against her, letting the tears run into her expensive blouse. He switched to the left buttock, inflicting the same stinging strokes. Nicola prayed that the left cheek would be the last, but when she felt a stinging crack on the top of her right leg her heart sank and she wailed in protest. Not another dozen on each leg, surely! The next smacked into the back of her left thigh, but then to her relief she heard the paddle being put on the table.

Rebecca let go and Carlo helped her up, holding her shaking body. Nicola was still crying fitfully and wouldn't look at him.

'Brava, Nicola,' he said. It was the first time he had used her name. He held her to him and she continued to cry on his shoulder. Rebecca brought her a glass of wine.

'I can't drink any more; I'm driving,' she said between sobs.

Rebecca smiled at her. 'Not tonight, you're not. You must stay here.'

As she sipped the wine Nicola thought about the whipping to come. She didn't see how she would be able to withstand it. Her buttocks already felt bruised and swollen. They must have had sixty strokes of the paddle. She wondered if they were the same dark cherry-red that Rebecca's were after James had dealt with them.

Carlo was still supporting her, then he carried her upstairs, where she could lie facedown on his bed while he rubbed some soothing lotion into her bottom. Nicola wondered what else he might have in mind, but she was too weak to resist any offer of rest. Sitting beside her on the bed he applied the cream with surprising gentleness. While he did so he praised her beauty and courage, speaking quietly, hypnotically.

'You deserve a whipping,' he said reflectively, 'but not tonight. I think your poor bottom needs time to heal.'

'It wasn't all my fault,' she protested. 'Why am I being punished so severely?' Carlo said nothing. 'I don't know whether I can take it,' she whispered into the wet pillow.

'You can. Follow Rebecca's example, how strong she was when you saw Sir James thrash her.'

He seemed to know a lot about all this, she thought. She was surprised how close Rebecca and Carlo were, considering they had only recently met. Perhaps their friendship had been consummated with an intimate spanking; not that they were likely to confide in her.

Carlo unhooked her bra and began to massage her back. It was sensual and relaxing. The ache in her bottom was subsiding, replaced by that sense of wellbeing she always felt in the aftermath of corporal punishment.

'When?' she sighed.

'Wednesday evening at seven,' he replied. They must have agreed this already. Perhaps Rebecca had just been trying to scare her by telling her it would be tonight.

Two weeks to the day since my sin in the gym, she thought.

After Edward's death she had longed for over a year to feel the discipline he gave her. Then came the opportunity with James. Now it seemed as if that one incident had opened the floodgates and she was to have a year's worth of beatings in less than a month.

Carlo didn't leave her that night. He made love to her in his marvellous Latin way in the single bed, careful not to press her tender arse. Then he slept on the floor next to the bed, to give her room to rest properly, and as she again walked up the path to the cottage she wondered how people who could be sexually sadistic could also be so gentle.

Nicola was not really sure why she had come back. It was true that she felt penitent, but Saturday's paddling could easily have been chastisement enough. A morbid curiosity nagged at her to know what the dreadful punishment of whipping would feel like. Most of all, however, she suspected it was the charismatic Carlo who drew her, and the gnawing intensity of incipient love.

Rebecca's greeting was friendly, but Nicola did not assume that all was forgiven. Carlo was in the sitting room and rose to kiss her on the cheek. The hostess excused herself to get drinks.

Nicola noticed a difference in the lamp-lit room: a chunky hook had been screwed into the central ceiling beam. Carlo shepherded her to the sofa, where he sat down. Nicola hesitated. He had indicated the seat next to him on the sofa, but the flogger lay there and he made no attempt to move it. When she picked it up and sat he asked her if the Italian leather felt good in her hands. His voice held the same hypnotic quality as before, and she ran her fingers through the three flat tails, each about eighteen inches long. They seemed so light and innocuous, but no doubt were less so when whirled through the air by a strong arm.

As she studied the whip closely Rebecca's lingering perfume was supplanted by the strong smell of new leather. Carlo took it from her and, holding the tails about halfway down, gently slapped her thigh with them.

'See, it does not hurt,' he said playfully.

'Will you promise to do it like that?' she asked with a weak smile, and in reply he just shook his head.

From time to time Nicola read spanking stories, in which the luckless heroines always told themselves to be strong, and on Saturday Carlo too had told her to be strong, like Rebecca. So, consoling herself that flogging would be preferable to another paddling, she told herself to be brave. Some faded bruises still troubled her after four days, and while the whip might be more stinging, she thought it would be less heavy than the paddle.

Rebecca reappeared with the wine, a deep red Barolo brought by Carlo. Nicola grimaced a little at its strength, but forced herself to drink more. The comfortable way in which Rebecca chatted to her seemed incongruous, knowing that Carlo was about to give her the beating of her life. No one hurried her and Nicola waited for the warmth of the wine to course through her body before finishing her glass.

Once she had done so Rebecca rose and collected something from the other side of the room. Carlo passed the whip to Nicola again and told her to kiss it, as it was about to kiss her. It was amazing, thought Nicola, how even such twaddle could sound sexy in an Italian accent. To humour him she pressed the tails of the implement to her lips.

Rebecca led her to the centre of the room and helped her undress completely, while Carlo watched. Even after Saturday Nicola was more nervous to be naked in front of him than any man before, but his admiring gaze gratified her.

When all her clothes had been neatly laid on the sofa Carlo fastened leather cuffs around Nicola's wrists; the cuffs linked by an adjustable strap. Then effortlessly he lifted her by the waist and she obediently slipped the strap over the hook, and when he released her she could only just reach the floor and she had to strain on tiptoe.

Powerlessly strung up like a bird at the butchers, Nicola felt a nervous excitement in the pit of her stomach. She was his helpless plaything. She could see herself in the mirror over the fireplace, her stretched torso heaving gently in anticipation. Carlo stood behind her, holding her hips and smiling at her in the mirror. She caught sight of Rebecca standing to one side, a determined look darkening her face. In spite of her fiery temper, Rebecca had always seemed to Nicola to be a kind woman, so did she have no qualms at forcing a girl to submit to such brutal treatment?

Carlo took off his light sweater, revealing his dark-haired chest and well-defined stomach. Swoon material, thought Nicola, wondering how he got those muscles lifting paint brushes all day.

Rebecca approached her and said, 'Once this is over I will be satisfied. If you like you may even stay on as James' secretary, although I would expect your work to be so good that he is never tempted to beat you again.'

Nicola nodded and Rebecca stepped back to leave plenty of room for Carlo's swing.

'Forty lashes, Nicola,' he said, running the thongs through his left hand. 'Added to the sixty with the paddle, it will bring your total sentence to one hundred strokes.'

Not knowing what even one lash felt like Nicola was deeply apprehensive, but she nodded her understanding. He explained that he would tolerate a little movement on the hook, but moving too much or too soon would lead to penalty strokes.

'There is one final thing,' he continued. 'After every fifth lash I expect you to say, "I am sorry, Rebecca". Failing to say it in a reasonable time will earn a penalty stroke.'

'Okay,' she mumbled.

'Speak up and tell me that you understand the instructions.'

Firmly she said, 'Yes, sir, I do.' Why had she called him sir? It just came out naturally. From nowhere, in the flick of a switch, he had become the dominant male in her life.

With trepidation she watched in the mirror as he moved his arm back for the first time. Then quickly he brought the whip from high above his head, snapping it into her bottom with a twist of his torso. Nicola gasped and blinked. Nothing had ever felt like that; it was like being slapped with a thousand stinging nettles. Before she had a chance to absorb the awful sensation he delivered the second lash, and the third. Her eyes were watering and she took gulps of breath. As the fourth and fifth strokes bit into her she began to whimper, tears rolling down her cheeks. The sharpness of the pain was unbelievable. There was a pause; she didn't know why. Her only thought was that she could never take the full forty. Then when she saw them looking at her expectantly she remembered.

'I'm sorry, Rebecca,' she said through her tears.

Carlo smoothed out the thongs and drew back for the next batch of strokes. As he proceeded Nicola's moans turned into shrieks, but he did not stop until after the tenth. Between shuddering breaths Nicola stammered out the apology again.

Soon she was arching her body forward as his arm fell, to try to avoid full contact with the whip's biting tails. As she did so for the third time he stopped his arm mid-air.

'A penalty stroke for moving,' he said coldly, and delivered a lash to the small of her back, provoking an astonished wail.

Nicola could not prevent herself from dodging the whip so Carlo asked Rebecca to blindfold her, and after taking a moment to steady the girl's sobbing Rebecca pulled a black band over her eyes. She smoothed Nicola's hair under the band, pushing the damp strands back behind her ears. Feeling Rebecca's gentle touch in the midst of her suffering made Nicola cry all the more, and the tears flooded into the band's absorbent felt.

Now Carlo varied the frequency of his delivery, so she could not guess when the strokes would fall. With each cut came an answering scream from Nicola. Sometimes, above her howling, she caught the whip's faint whistle, but she barely had time to flinch her buttocks before the thongs wrapped around them, sending her dancing from foot to foot. Her knees began to buckle, causing her to swing on the hook. Her arms and shoulders ached from supporting her weight.

Another pause - had they reached twenty? She could no longer see if they were expecting her to speak. She was perspiring and breathing deeply, as if working out. After a moment she risked blurting out the apology, expecting the next blow to land soon after, but instead Rebecca's scent wafted near again and a glass was put to her lips.

'We're halfway through,' she said. 'Rest a moment and have a sip of wine.' Although Nicola coughed up the first drops, the glass was held patiently to her mouth until she had taken several good sips. When her foot slipped some wine spilled down her chin and instinctively she apologised. Rebecca told her not to worry, dabbing her face with a handkerchief to dry both wine and tears.

Although the warmth of the wine brought her some comfort, her bum felt lacerated beyond repair. She despaired to think that she had to bear the same amount over again.

'Let me down, I don't think I can take any more,' she pleaded, hoping for the woman's mercy, but there was no sound of a reprieve.

Instead she felt the whip's handle stroking her shoulder blades. Carlo traced the shape of her back until he reached the stinging flesh of her bottom. He cupped the lower curve of each buttock in his hands. Surprisingly the skin here was not so sore, and Nicola realised he had been working his strokes steadily down from the upper slope of her backside.

'Now for here and here,' he said, patting the underside of her buttocks and the backs of her legs.

'No more sexy miniskirts for a while, Nicola,' Rebecca could not resist goading.

The second half of the punishment was almost

unbearable. When the thongs sliced into her legs her body lurched and swung so erratically that Carlo struggled to land the strokes on target. During one pause, her mind blanked by pain, she forgot to utter the apology, and such failures of compliance were dealt with ruthlessly, with penalty lashes to her lower back.

Finally Carlo called Rebecca over to hold the girl steady, while he flogged the roundness of her bottom once more. Nicola wanted to faint; and perhaps she did because she found herself with her arms around Carlo's neck, her hands still cuffed. She looked him in the face through half closed eyes.

'I'm sorry, Rebecca,' she murmured, but Carlo told her that Rebecca had left and they were alone.

Deep into the night Carlo slept naked beside Nicola on Rebecca's double bed. As she watched him her mind was a strange mixture of thoughts, some silly and some solemn. He had eagerly inflicted on her the utmost agony of her life, but it was eventually followed by ecstasy and she was left in no doubt about her feelings for Carlo.

Chapter 9

Spotless table linen, glittering chandeliers and subtle blue decor formed the backdrop of the evening in the Dorchester ballroom. A small string orchestra played softly in the background, and groups of people dressed in a cosmopolitan mixture of costly evening wear had begun to drift in from the reception hall and take their seats. There was an air of genteel gaiety.

As he entered, James was deep in conversation with the head of Scotland Yard's Art and Antiques Unit. The detective, who held a relatively junior grade in the hierarchy of the Metropolitan Police, felt rather honoured to be invited to this event at all. At dinner he would sit at the table of the Commissioner himself, along with other members of the Met's top team. He listened to James attentively, although his eyes were following his wife, who was chatting excitedly with an exotic redhead some feet in front. Their invitation to the ball, which he suspected was the work of Sir James, had seriously put him in her good books. He was pretty sure he would get lucky at home tonight.

In the reception hall the sounds of seasonal jollity were more muted as the crowd thinned. Well-starched waiters, who had moved to and fro with champagne and other aperitifs, began to clear away the debris. Rebecca and senior figures from her firm moved easily between the groups, oiling the cogs of social interaction.

As she cast her eyes about for stragglers Rebecca noticed a stag group of young high flyers, including a senior civil servant from the Department for Culture, Media and Sport. She was taken aback to find that Nicola was at the centre of this select band, listening attentively to the young men and saying the odd word in reply. Whatever she had just said was obviously pertinent, because the mandarin nodded energetically before continuing his flow.

Rebecca flushed with pleasure; Nicola was full of surprises. She looked ravishing in a black gown with simple lines, finished off by a pearl necklace and earrings. Rebecca realised that she knew very little about the girl. Indeed, before this week she had been polite to her but distant. She knew that Nicola had been the ward of James' old friend, but that did not make her any happier at seeing the girl flaunt her body around his office. But the previous night they had spent the evening together and their relationship flowed into much warmer waters.

Carlo, who'd been caught up in a group of artists arguing about the merits of various exhibitions over the past year, appeared at Rebecca's elbow.

'You need to rescue your date from her new fans,' she said, nodding towards Nicola's group, and he moved off in pursuit.

As Carlo drew out the chair for Nicola, James was taking his seat opposite them.

'James, someone's just told me that the gallery we visited in London has been closed by the police,' she said excitedly. 'Francesco's, wasn't it called? Did you know?'

Carlo stiffened immediately and James glanced at him. 'Yes, I think someone mentioned it,' he replied airily. 'Good job I didn't buy that Madonna and Child, isn't it?' This time he studiously avoided looking at Carlo.

'I thought it was a dirty, horrible painting

anyway,' she laughed, surprised to notice Carlo lapse into silence. Sensing competition from the cocks in the reception hall he had plumed himself to respond to the challenge, becoming animated and attentive. He had whisked her away from the group, which looked on enviously, resenting in their staid English way the easy gallantry of the Italian. Now, suddenly, the taciturn Carlo had made a comeback, and Nicola reflected that her date was the moodiest man she had ever met.

The remaining guests at their table arrived, under Rebecca's escort. To Nicola's left sat an elderly professor from the Courtauld Institute of Art and his wife. On Carlo's right sat the wife of a leading investment banker, her husband next to Rebecca.

Nicola chatted affably with the professor who, it transpired, had known Edward slightly, and she suspected that this happy coincidence was a victory for Rebecca's skilful handling of the seating plans. When the professor went on to express his admiration for one of Edward's scholarly books, Nicola was delighted. She rewarded him with such kittenish behaviour that by the end of the meal he was a flushed and happy old man.

From time to time Rebecca glanced across at this performance with admiration. Nicola was proving herself to be so adept socially that she was sorry the girl would soon be leaving. Rebecca herself was in conversation with the banker about the buzz of the moment, the closure of Francesco's. The banker was sharing, in a carrying voice, gossip about the police raid. Although the police had soon finished their investigation at the scene, Francesco had not yet reopened his gallery. It was rumoured that the mistrust which would now surround him might lead him to sell up. Carlo, she could see, was more interested in this conversation than in entertaining his own neighbour at the table.

The banker's wife wanted to bore him with accounts of her visits to Italy. Carlo was fending her off by pretending to understand little English, but the woman was having none of it. Moving in the shrewd world of her husband's financial wizardry she was well able to see through the ploys of a penniless artist. Whilst her tales purported to cover the many museums and classical sites they had visited, Carlo was actually given more detail about the luxury hotels and yachts where they had stayed.

Both Rebecca and Nicola noticed that the banker's wife was not Carlo's only admirer. Their young waitress had made several bright-eyed glances towards him, and when she finally caught his eye she gave him a dazzling smile. As she served his vegetables her arm touched his, and her cleavage lingered as long as possible near his face. Her blonde hair was swept back from her shapely neck and forehead into a short ponytail. Her black skirt was shorter and tighter than those of the other waitresses and showed every curve of her bottom. As she moved off Carlo gave it a cursory glance, but in his glumness he did not seem interested. Rebecca and Nicola smiled and shared raised eyebrows across the table.

On Thursday Nicola was too sore and aching to go to work, so she phoned James to say she felt unwell. Ever the gentleman he was solicitous and hoped she would be recovered by Friday night. So, thought Nicola, did she, or else dancing would be a nightmare.

Rebecca had gone up to London the previous night to oversee final preparations for the ball. It was an important event in her firm's calendar, bolstering their connections with the rich and influential and fostering new ones. She didn't return until the evening, so Carlo and Nicola had the day to themselves.

They went to the village pub for lunch and then for a walk in the countryside. He told her about growing up in Calabria. He spoke warmly of the Mediterranean light and the wind off the Ionian Sea.

'If you love it so much why did you leave?' she asked.

He replied vaguely that after his mother's death he wanted a change of location, and that rich art patrons abounded more in Lombardy than in the poorer south. It seemed explanation enough, yet the way he said it suggested to Nicola that there had been other reasons.

In turn she told him about her life in Oxford; how sometimes she had felt as though she didn't belong there, because it was a place full of brilliant minds. So much of the city revolved around the life of the university that nonacademics were treated rather as an afterthought. Still, she wanted to show off its beauties to him. It was one of only a tiny number of places in Britain where a large medieval centre had been preserved. She promised to take him soon.

When darkness fell at four o'clock they returned to the cottage. Once again Carlo applied lotion to her body and once again it culminated in marvellous sex. Afterwards he begged her to come to Milan with him. He knew the way they had met would not make it easy for them, but he told her that he loved her and wanted them to try.

Nicola had to admit that a boyfriend who paddled her on the first date and whipped her on the second did not look like a keeper. Yet she was sure she loved Carlo too, or at least was infatuated with him enough to call it love. She was happy and a little surprised when he said he loved her, and wondered if he meant it or if it was just specious Italian charm. On the other hand, if he just regarded her as a brief affair why burden himself by giving her houseroom? Their relationship seemed to be moving too quickly, but given the geography, thought Nicola, if it didn't move quickly it would never move at all.

And then there was James. She accepted that that had ended now. There were some sizzling memories, but his future lay with Rebecca. If she stayed on to work for him there would always be tensions between the three of them. So she accepted Carlo's offer to give him and Milan a chance. It was exciting and new, and if it turned sour she could simply come home.

When Rebecca returned at seven she sent Carlo to have a long drink at the pub, explaining that she needed to talk dresses with Nicola. Eventually the two girls did discuss their clothes for the ball, but it seemed that Rebecca had some serious apologising to do first. She was sorry for having had Nicola punished so severely, and said that she herself deserved to receive Nicola's punishment, but James, the one man she desired to deliver it, must never know what happened.

'Even though you were wrong to sleep with him it didn't warrant a whipping,' she said contritely, holding Nicola's hands. 'Will you forgive me?'

As well as forgiveness Nicola suspected that Rebecca was looking for a promise never to reveal the events to James, and Nicola's reply stopped short of granting her that.

'I will forgive you,' she said, 'and if it's any consolation, I never actually slept with James; we just had a quickie.'

'A quickie? That's not like James,' Rebecca said ironically.

'Well, okay, it wasn't that quick, but it was only the once.'

Rebecca seemed somewhat satisfied, and hugged the girl. Of course, thought Nicola, her concerns would be much allayed now that she and Carlo were an item. She never really believed James would spurn such a lovely and accomplished woman as Rebecca for her, a mere girl, even though older men behaved oddly with young women sometimes.

If James had wanted to get serious about her,

would Nicola have felt the same, she wondered? She didn't know. It would have been a tempting offer for a girl all alone in the world.

'I want to thank you for coming to the ball, even though you must be feeling so sore,' said Rebecca.

'I'm dying to go,' lied Nicola enthusiastically

'Do you need a dress?' asked Rebecca. 'We're similar sizes.'

Nicola shook her head. 'Edward bought me a special one for his last college ball. I think I'll wear that. Fortunately it's off the shoulder, not backless.'

'Have you any jewellery?'

'Not really. I've some rings and bracelets my mother left me. My parents weren't well off.'

Rebecca fetched a white box from her bedroom. 'I'll lend you these for the night, if you like.'

Nicola handled the beautiful pearl necklace and earrings. 'Are you kidding?'

'No, of course not. Put them on.'

Nicola was beginning to enjoy the warmer, more relaxed Rebecca. Although not fond of her methods, deep down she admired her for fighting to keep James. They settled down in the living room with some wine and chatted about James and Carlo. When Rebecca asked if she could call her Nick, she readily agreed.

'And should I call you Becks?' she asked impishly.

'Not unless you want another paddling,' laughed Rebecca.

'Was James the first man to spank you?' asked Nicola. She couldn't imagine the daunting

Rebecca allowing many men to reprimand her.

'No, it was my cousin, Mark. I was sixteen and I was crazy about him. I flirted shamelessly. Real hussy stuff. But he wouldn't play ball. He was training to be a doctor and quoted statistics about the higher rate of congenital deformity in children whose parents are first cousins.'

'How romantic!' Nicola cried sardonically.

'I suppose he was right, but I wasn't planning to have kids by him. I just wanted to lose my virginity.' Rebecca mused a while. 'He looked a bit like an English version of Carlo. He was very serious; always worrying about people in poor countries. He was so different to the other boys I knew.'

'How did he come to spank you?' prompted Nicola.

'He was going to Oxford medical school and he came to stay with us before term started. For some reason he couldn't stay in his college for the first couple of weeks. It was still my summer holidays so we were alone together most days. With both my parents at work I could torment him to my heart's content. I walked round the house half naked and I was always brushing my hair near him. I could see his sneaky glances so I knew he found me sexy, but he thought I was shallow because I didn't know anything about the genocide in Rwanda.

'That summer Nelson Mandela had been elected President of South Africa with loads of fuss in the media, so I asked Mark to tell me what was so great about him. He was sitting on the sofa so he could have all his books on the seat next to him. I pushed them out of the way and sat down. I was wearing a short summer dress. I kicked off my shoes and sat with my legs under me, careful to make sure most of my thighs were bare.'

'And you ended up over his knee?'

'No, not then. He was so animated about Mandela I hadn't the heart to be too provocative. But I edged closer for a kiss. He knew what I was doing, and when I got close enough I dived in to kiss him but he dodged me and jumped to his feet. "It's not right, Becky", he said, but I saw the tent in his trousers so I reckoned it was only a matter of time.'

'What happened next?' Nicola was riveted.

'Next day I went for a run. Instead of my normal jogging kit I wore my strip from the school athletics team: tight black shorts and a blue top which left plenty of bare midriff. I didn't tire myself out though, because the exercise I wanted was after the run. When I got back I could hear music playing on the radio in his bedroom. Now or never, I thought, and when I opened the door he was lying on the bed reading.

'"I've just been for a run, so I'm going for a shower", I said. He didn't say a word, just looked up at me. I took my top off. I had a black sports bra underneath. My shorts were high-cut so there was usually a fair bit of lower cheek exposed, but I'd run them into my bum crack so that most of the cheeks were bare. As I said, I was really slutty. I turned round in the doorway and let him have a good look before going to my own room. My stomach was all butterflies. I waited to see if he would come. He didn't, so I took off my bra and was about to go back into his room when he appeared at my door and grabbed my arm.

'"This has got to stop now, Becky", he said. He sat on my bed, dragged me over his knee and gave me a really good spanking. To him it probably seemed like a punishment, but he was acting out my most frequent fantasy. Although my shorts were on my bum cheeks were bare anyway, so I got a good feel of the palm of his hand. When he stopped I was really tingling and ready for him. I asked him why he didn't take my shorts down and do a proper job of it, and in reply he pulled me up and fetched the hairbrush from my dressing table. He made me bend over the foot of the bed and kept slapping me with it. Eventually I couldn't stop myself. I put my hand down my shorts and started to masturbate. He stopped hitting me, but I just stayed bent over until I'd finished. Thinking about it later things might have been different if I'd turned as soon as the spanks stopped. I don't really know why I didn't. Just inexperience, I suppose. When I eventually turned round he was staring at me with an enormous erection in his pants. I unzipped him and gave him a blowjob. It was my first time, and even though it wasn't what I'd planned, it was just as erotic. Afterwards he went back to his room and I had a shower.'

'Did your parents ever find out?' asked Nicola, breathlessly.

'No. He was very quiet that night at dinner so I thought they might guess something had happened, but actually they were pretty caught up in their careers in those days, so they often didn't notice things at home.

'For the next few days he made sure he was out most of the time at the library. Then his college room became available, so he left us.'

'Do you ever see him now?'

'After he qualified he went off to do a year with Oxfam in Africa. He was hacked to death by robbers stealing the medical supplies.'

Nicola was aghast. 'Oh my God! That's so awful!'

'And of course he had avoided me like the plague after that summer, so I never had a chance to apologise. When I grew up and realised life wasn't just about girly fun all the time, I would have loved just to be friends with him.'

Rebecca's eyes had taken on a distant look, and Nicola pressed her hand.

'We never cry in our family, but I wept buckets at his funeral. I think my parents were ashamed of me.'

Being entrusted with this intimate incident from Rebecca's past made Nicola feel much closer to her. She wanted to stay on and talk, but at that moment Carlo came in from the pub.

After the meal the lights were dimmed and the string orchestra gave way to a dance band. Nicola and Rebecca used the brief lull to escape to the ladies' room.

'Do you think we can trust James and Carlo alone with that waitress?' asked Nicola.

'I doubt it. That minx is a spanking waiting to happen,' Rebecca laughed. 'By the way,' she continued, 'that tall blond guy from the DCMS you were speaking to over drinks - he's leaving the civil service to stand for Parliament. He's tipped to be a future cabinet minister, at the very least.'

'Wow, I didn't know how honoured I was,' laughed Nicola. Then her tone grew serious.

'Listen, there's something important I need to tell you.' She related her plan to go to Milan with Carlo. Rebecca was astonished; she hadn't realised things had gone so far between them.

'But are you sure? We know so little about him.' For a while Rebecca tried to persuade her to delay her decision.

'I know there's a risk, but in my heart I feel it's right,' said Nicola.

'What about the language?'

'I speak holiday Italian. My guardian spent summers dragging me round ancient ruins. I expect it'll improve quickly under Carlo's tuition.'

'What will you do for a job? We have contacts there. It's a long shot, but there may be something.'

'Thanks. If you could ask them it would be great.'

'What about his...?' Rebecca stopped. Other women had come into the room so they left it, and in the corridor outside Nicola picked up her point.

'We had a long talk yesterday, and I told him there would be days when I wanted to be able to sit down without my bottom aching,' she said dryly. 'He promised never to whip me again, but we agreed he can punish me less severely when I'm a bad girl.'

'And how often will you be a bad girl?' laughed Rebecca.

Nicola mused for a moment. 'Every four to six weeks, I think.'

The sight of two beautiful women giggling together gladdened the hearts of the men they passed on the way back to the ball.

While Rebecca was circulating Carlo amongst various bigwigs, James asked Nicola to dance. They glided happily about the floor until James' hand caught one of the weals on her back. Nicola grimaced and James looked at her with concern.

'I'm sorry, did I catch your foot?'

She told him it was minor back problem, but when it happened again he insisted on knowing the details and her weak cover story began to fall apart under his probing. When he tested his suspicions by pressing his right hand into her bottom she flinched. James insisted on examining her. After all, he told her, this would affect the remaining punishment session which had yet to be rearranged. So reluctantly she took him to her hotel room, where he had her take off her dress. Standing in her black lingerie she watched him in the mirror as he ran his fingers along the livid stripes on her legs, buttocks and back. He was horrified and wanted to know who had done it, and when she told him it led to more questions.

'But why?'

'I begged him to,' she said

'You begged a stranger to whip you?' James sounded incredulous. 'Why on earth would you do that?'

'I... I felt guilty about us. It was a form of penitence.'

James did not sound at all convinced. 'And why Carlo?'

'I guessed he was cruel enough to do a good job,' she replied, not adding that he was also sexy and mesmerising.

'Where was Rebecca when this was happening?' he asked suspiciously.

'In London, arranging the ball,' Nicola lied. She wanted to protect Rebecca but felt guilty about lying to James.

His eyes narrowed. 'There's something you're not telling me.'

She was silent, knowing how bad she was at lying and not wanting to say too much. Instead she tried another direction.

'You know you and I wouldn't work out,' she said, her voice breaking. 'You're engaged to a beautiful and successful woman.'

'Always tears with you, Nick,' said James. 'Playing the damsel in distress while you twist us all round your little finger.'

Nicola was mortified that James thought so badly of her.

'No, it's not like that!' She looked imploringly at him, but he did not relent.

'Well you may find you're scheming yourself into trouble.'

'What do you mean?' she asked.

'What do you really know of Carlo; his life in Italy, his friends and associates?'

'I know I love him.'

'Love him? You've only just met him,' James snorted angrily.

'I need a new direction. Carlo feels right.'

'What you need is some sense spanked into you. Remember our agreement lets me spank you whenever I want to.'

'Spank me then, if you must,' she said defiantly. She was exasperated and frustrated. Everyone always thought she was in the wrong.

'Come here,' he said menacingly, throwing off his dinner jacket. He sat on the foot of the bed and pulled her across his lap. She yelped in protest at his roughness, but he settled her waist snugly over his thighs and held her in place with his left forearm. She stretched her hands to the floor to support herself. With his right hand he pushed her thighs down so that her knees were bent and her bottom spread to its fullest extent. She dug the tips of her shoes into the carpet to hold her position.

'Are you comfortable?' he snapped.

'Am I supposed to be comfortable?' she snapped back.

In answer he brought his hand down sharply on her right buttock. Then he paused and caressing her whole bottom. Was he suddenly reluctant to whack her existing welts? He wasn't. He slipped her panties down her legs and set to work. At first he spanked her alternately on each buttock at a fast pace. Then he switched to slower, harder strokes across the centre of her bottom. She winced as the old bruises were smacked anew, but she made little sound apart from the occasional 'ouch'. Being spanked by James felt good.

Finally he stopped, but neither of them moved. She was wet and she could feel he was hard, but this time they could do nothing about it.

'I would like to have gone on much longer, but we'll be missed,' he said quietly. He didn't sound angry any more.

For a minute or two they stayed silently as they were, then sombrely he said, 'So you *are* into Italian primitives, after all.'

'I was falling for you, James,' she said, still facing the carpet. More confessions over his knee, she thought. 'After what happened between us I can't stay on with you. It wouldn't be fair to Rebecca.'

He lifted her up gently then left her to re-do her make up and dress before returning to the ball.

Back in the ballroom the tables were sparsely populated but the dance floor was full. There was no sign of Carlo and Rebecca, but Nicola could see the professor and his wife dancing contentedly together. His wife was beaming at him. Perhaps Nicola's attentive treatment had rejuvenated him. She felt she could do with some rejuvenation herself, and something to ease her latest bout of bottom bashing. She sat down cautiously. The waitress appeared and she ordered a vodka and tonic. The banker's wife, whose name was Audrey, was the only other person at the table.

'You look a little saddle sore, dear,' the woman

said. 'Have you been out riding today?'

'No, but I've had some hard workouts this week.'

'Oh, the gym. I hate it, but I have to go. Otherwise I'd need to live on lettuce.'

Audrey asked if Carlo was her partner. She replied that he was, but soon regretted it because the woman immediately became inquisitive. Nicola felt foolish in being unable to answer many of her questions about him, and in the end she had to admit that they had met only a week before.

'I saw one of his paintings in a shop in Milan,' said Audrey. 'His stroke work is very energetic.'

'It can be,' agreed Nicola. At least that was one aspect of Carlo she felt qualified to talk about.

A young man appeared at her side and asked her to dance, saving her from further displays of ignorance. He was from the group she had mingled with before dinner, and although she was glad to escape Audrey's re-run of the Spanish Inquisition, she was not looking forward to further torture on the dance floor.

In the end it wasn't so bad, because the music had moved into the modern era and most couples were happy to dance apart. After her first partner came a succession of the other men she had met in the reception room, ending in the future cabinet minister himself. Nicola found herself flirting with him.

'Aren't you too good-looking to be Prime Minister?' she asked. He smiled modestly and asked if she would answer a personal question. He was so polite and had such a ready smile that she immediately felt able to open up to him, although she knew what was coming.

'Are you really with that artist?'

'Yes, I'm afraid so. I'm going to Milan with him.'

'I've changed my mind about being Prime Minister,' he said solemnly. 'I want to be the Ambassador to Italy instead.' Nicola knew it was corny, but she liked it all the same.

As they left the dance floor James appeared with someone at his elbow. Her dancing partner greeted James deferentially, and politely asked after his fiancée before excusing himself. James turned to her.

'Nick, this chap had been pestering me to introduce you to him. Would you mind?'

James seemed to have perked up since their last encounter. She thought several scotches may have had something to do with it, although he was far from drunk.

'This chap' turned out to be a world famous sculptor of the Brit Art movement, and though Nicola knew little about art she was an avid fan of the celebrity gossip magazines which featured his exploits from time to time.

'Gosh, yes, I'd be delighted,' she said in astonishment. It was clear that the awe in her voice pandered to the artist's vanity, and she soon found herself on the dance floor again.

The tunes had moved back in time to traditional waltzes once more, so contact was inevitable. Nicola was determined not to grimace, so she fixed her smile and forced herself through it. The artist was a little tipsy, but he was light on his feet and handled her gently. After escorting her to her table he cheekily slipped his card into her purse and begged her to call him one day soon.

Audrey's husband had returned and inevitably he too wanted to claim a dance with Nicola. He was such a boorish and heavy-handed man that she didn't bother to hide her discomfort as they waltzed. Fortunately he was so certain that his billions bought him limitless sex appeal that he noticed nothing amiss.

Nicola was reprieved from further dancing when the floor was temporarily cleared for the results of a charity auction to be announced. She was thrilled to see a minor member of royalty appear, amid a bevy of aides and photographers. As he swept by he nodded greetings to several people, including James, who gracefully bowed his head in response. Nicola was impressed, but wondered what the royal would have thought of James had he been in her hotel room an hour before. But knowing her recent luck, she decided, she would probably have had to take a turn across both their laps.

He made a short speech about the charity, art therapy for victims of serious injury, of which he was patron, and shook hands with the winners. As the dancing resumed Nicola watched him share a few words with various VIPs before being whisked off to his next engagement. It was a life that needed stamina, she thought.

At the end of the evening Carlo reappeared having done the rounds of rich clients with Rebecca. He still seemed morose, and later Rebecca told her that she had been none too pleased by his manners, but since artists were expected to be moody it had probably done him no harm. Nicola flushed with pride when Rebecca added that if she were to stick with Carlo her social skills could help his career.

Determined to dance with him at least once she dragged him to the floor, and as James and Rebecca followed them she overheard their conversation. Rebecca was pleased she'd not once caught James ogling the waitress' obvious charms.

'My hands are full with your bottom,' he replied urbanely.

'Yes, especially when they're giving it a good walloping,' she giggled.

'I'd love you even if we didn't do that,' he said seriously.

'I wouldn't have it any other way,' said Rebecca, pressing herself against him.

Nicola clung to Carlo, wondering what James had meant when he asked what she really knew of Carlo's associates. He held her tightly, seeming in his distraction to have forgotten that her body was still tender. The band played *Bewitched, Bothered and Bewildered*, which, thought Nicola, described her condition exactly.

Chapter 10

On the Monday following the ball Rebecca took Nicola to lunch. She told James they would need a couple of hours because she wanted to speak earnestly to Nicola about Carlo. She wanted to reassure herself yet again that Nicola knew what she would be taking on. James readily fell in with her plan. Rebecca knew he disliked Carlo and was appalled at the thought of Nicola running off to Italy with him.

The two women were sitting at a small table in a busy bistro in the town. Outside a grey chill hung over the bustling streets of Henley, but inside the atmosphere was warm and infused with the smell of French cooking. Nicola ate a vegetarian quiche in crisp pastry, while Rebecca had mussels, neatly scooping them out with the other half of the shell. They each had a glass of white wine. Although there were only three days to go until Christmas the place was blessedly free of rowdy groups with paper hats and party poppers.

'You were a smash hit at the ball, Nick.'

'Really?' Nicola was pleasantly surprised.

'Lots of men asked about you, including our chief exec, and I got all the kudos for discovering you.' Rebecca grinned.

'I like the idea of being "discovered",' laughed Nicola. 'It makes me sound important.'

Inevitably their conversation soon turned to the men in their pasts. They were both anxious to pick up from where they'd been interrupted the previous Thursday night.

'It's so hard finding someone who will...' Nicola didn't finish her sentence but Rebecca knew exactly what she meant.

'Tell me about it. But don't throw yourself on Carlo just because of great sex. I'm beginning to realise he has a shady past.'

'I can sense he has a dark side, but at the moment it makes him more desirable. But maybe the fever will pass and I'll be free of it and come home.'

Rebecca questioned her more deeply, seeking to confirm how far the girl's feelings for him went, and what he may have told her about his life. In the end she had to accept that Nicola's mind was made up: Carlo was a risk she was willing to take. And whatever doubts hung over him there was one aspect of Carlo's character which made him an ideal companion for Nicola.

'You know, it took me ages to find a man to handle me properly,' said Rebecca. 'So now I've got James I'm determined to keep him.'

'I can vouch for that,' said Nicola, with feeling.

Rebecca told her some funny stories about her early attempts to goad her boyfriends into spanking her. Her tantrums had tormented them so badly that Nicola felt sorry for them. On one occasion she had been reduced to stealing some money from a boyfriend's wallet and then owning up to it. He was so dopey that he immediately forgave her, but she insisted that he must not let her off scot-free.

'It's so humiliating to have to climb over a man's lap and plead "I'm a naughty girl, spank me",' complained Rebecca.

A young man at the next table glanced at them with interest, but his girlfriend did not look pleased.

'Shh,' giggled Nicola, 'you're embarrassing me!'

'You must have had the same problem.'

'Yes, I've found loads of men who loved my arse,' Nicola whispered, 'but not many who wanted to give it a good hiding. I had high hopes of one guy, Steven. He couldn't take his hands of it; fondling it, patting it, slapping it. But when we finally had sex it turned out he wanted...'

Nicola paused and glanced to see if their neighbour was still eavesdropping, before going on. 'You know, to do it up the bum.'

'Ooh... what's that like?' Rebecca was curious.

Nicola wrinkled her nose to show that she could take it or leave it, then went on to relate another incident in which she arranged for her boyfriend to find her flicking herself on the bottom with one of his leather belts. When he asked her what she was doing she told him it was good for her circulation.

'He didn't buy it. He thought I was kinky, but he did whack me quite hard with the belt and he was stunned with the sex afterwards.'

The young couple at the next table had finished, and the girl gave them a baleful glance as she left.

I know what you need, thought Rebecca, looking after her. I just hope your boyfriend does too.

They talked about using contact websites to find people. Neither had tried them but both had heard unsatisfactory reports from friends. It seemed that cyberspace made men bigger liars than they were already. They were rarely as young, as handsome or as solvent as they claimed to be.

'Somehow it doesn't feel right,' said Nicola. 'I

want to know something about a person and feel comfortable with them in the flesh before I reveal my innermost desires.'

Rebecca agreed. 'And our particular needs could be dangerous in the wrong hands.'

'Don't you think we're freaks?' asked Nicola.

'Freaks? Absolutely not. Why?'

'Because of what we like,' said Nicola

'It's common. Watch.' The waitress was just bringing their deserts, and Rebecca asked her, 'Does your boyfriend spank you?'

The young girl blushed, giving them their answer, before verbally confirming it. 'Yes, sometimes.'

Rebecca followed up, 'And do you like it?'

'Yes,' replied the girl.

'Why don't you ask him to cane you?' asked Rebecca.

'What? No way!' The horrified waitress hurried away and the two women laughed.

'Well, maybe we are a wee bit special,' admitted Rebecca, and then she related the story of her first caning from James.

'Even after I'd given my prettiest apology he still took me to his study and caned me. Oh, how my pussy cheered when he told me what he was going to do.' She sighed with pleasure at the memory. 'I begged him not to, of course, but he wouldn't give in to me.'

As the tables around them had emptied Nicola became more confiding. She divulged the story of her arrangement with Edward. There were many details she had kept from James, and she asked

Rebecca never to tell them to anyone. Rebecca was entranced by the tale of the whipping bench and the experimental clothing, and Edward's doomed relationship with Nicola's mother fascinated her. Edward had died before Rebecca had known James, so she'd never met him. She would have found his scholarship, his self-control in handling Nicola's sexuality and his ability to supply a wicked beating an irresistible combination.

'I would have married him like a shot,' she said, astonished that he had been a bachelor all his life. It was clear her words pleased her young friend.

Rebecca was finding that she enjoyed Nicola's company more and more. It helped that the younger girl plainly looked up to her and was impressed by her successful career, but there was something more important. Being with someone who so closely shared her sexual tastes gave her a tremendous feeling of release. For whatever she had said at the bistro she knew they were different from most women; the extreme treatment they craved set them apart. All in all she would miss Nicola and she was sorry they'd not had more time to be friends.

As they entered the gates of James' mansion Rebecca recognised the blue car parked at the door. It was the small Ford rented for Carlo's use, and she asked Nicola if she expected Carlo to be there. The girl shook her head.

'Perhaps he's here to see you,' she suggested.

'I don't think so,' replied Rebecca. 'He thinks I'm

in London.'

She drove quietly up the drive and stopped some distance short of the house. Then she took off her heels and started to run over the frosty lawn, beckoning Nicola to follow. Avoiding the study windows the two went round the back of the house to the kitchen, where the maid let them in and gave them a towel to wipe their damp feet.

'My toes are frozen,' grumbled Nicola. 'What's all this about?'

'Just follow me, and keep quiet.' Rebecca bustled Nicola out of the kitchen, telling the maid not to let on to Sir James that they had arrived. The maid solemnly promised not to, and carried on with her work indifferent to their cloak and dagger antics.

Rebecca hurried them upstairs and along a landing. They entered a tiny windowless room, which contained only a small desk and a chair. A number of electronic gadgets were fitted to one wall, and on the desk was a computer with a large monitor. Rebecca sat at the desk and switched it on. A moment or so after keying in a password the monitor became a split screen television, showing the rooms and grounds of the house. Rebecca selected the study for full screen viewing and switched on the sound.

James' voice emerged from the speakers. He was berating Carlo.

'Why did you beat her so harshly?'

Carlo seemed to resent being spoken to in this way. 'It is a matter between her and me, Sir James,' he said indignantly. 'Anyway, it was not so harsh.'

'I saw the marks,' said James with emphasis. This was news to Rebecca. She looked at Nicola questioningly, and the girl nodded and lowered her eyes. Nicola knelt beside Rebecca's chair and the two watched tensely as the scene unfolded.

After a moment's hesitation Carlo explained that Nicola had pleaded for her beating. She wanted to atone for seducing James and endangering Rebecca's engagement to him. James grumpily conceded that his story matched what Nicola had told him. Rebecca looked again at the girl, this time squeezing her hand in gratitude.

'You need to exercise some restraint when you discipline a woman,' James said crossly. 'This isn't the Dark Ages.'

'I'll remind him of that next time he whacks the living daylights out of me,' murmured Rebecca.

'Sir James, have you called me here to discuss my love life?' asked Carlo bluntly. 'It's really none of your business.'

'No, I asked you here because I know about the forged Cimabue.'

Carlo looked stunned. At first he said nothing, and then not very convincingly he blustered, 'I don't know what you mean.'

Direct as always, James was having none of the young man's prevarication. 'I found it in the back of Rebecca's portrait. It was very similar to another I've seen recently.'

'Is it still there?' Carlo asked innocently.

'No,' said James, 'and you are the only person who could have moved it.'

'If it is not there you have no evidence, Sir James.'

'I have photographs of the picture in its hiding place. If it were ever to come to market I would take them to the police.'

'I see,' said Carlo.

'I believe you forged both paintings, Carlo.'

Carlo did not reply.

'Apparently...' began James. He was finding it difficult to speak. 'Apparently Nicola has feelings for you. Young women are often poor judges of character in men.'

'You seem to have determined my character on very short acquaintance,' Carlo retorted hotly.

James must have seen the justice of this comment, because his manner became less belligerent. 'Perhaps, but the point is that Nicola's wellbeing has become very important to me.'

In the security room Nicola flushed.

'I don't want her mixed up with criminals,' James continued.

'I am not a criminal,' insisted Carlo.

James ignored this unlikely statement. 'Can you extricate yourself from the people you're involved with?'

'It's not that easy,' sighed Carlo.

'Who are they?' persisted James.

'Sir James, if I told you it would not be good for you, for me or for Nicola.'

James waited patiently, and at last Carlo said, 'There is an important man in Milan. He runs a syndicate. They were to get the proceeds from the sale of the forgeries.'

'They can't blame you, surely. The police have prevented the sale now.'

'They blame who they want. And those people tend to die, *dolorosamente*.'

'But if the paintings have not been sold how can they expect the money from you?'

'You do not understand, Sir James, I already owe them the money. The paintings would have paid my debt.'

'Gambling? Drugs?'

'No.'

'What then?'

'It is a family matter. I will not tell you more.'

James was staring out of the window, presumably wondering what was to be done. He turned back to Carlo and raised a question that had already struck Rebecca.

'If this syndicate is as powerful as you suggest, I don't understand their involvement. These paintings would sell for peanuts in comparison with the takings of organised crime.'

'These two are just part of a much bigger racket. There are other forgeries, thefts, smuggling...'

Carlo lapsed into a morose silence, presumably contemplating death *dolorosa*. James returned to the window. The girls waited expectantly for him to come to a decision.

'How much do you owe?' he asked at last.

'Sixty thousand Euros.'

'If you promise to stop producing fakes I will pay it.'

Carlo's head shot up in astonishment.

'I don't understand, Sir James. You want to pay

my debt for me?'

'What I propose is, I will pay you that sum to paint a wedding portrait of Rebecca,' explained James. 'This time one we can hang in the drawing room. Of course, I'll need to confirm it with Rebecca,' he added.

Carlo cheered up immensely. 'That is very generous,' he said warmly. 'I suppose you do it for Nicola and not for me.'

'You suppose correctly. Nicola was alone in the world. Now I regard her as...' he paused. 'As a daughter. I will be very angry if she comes to even the slightest harm in your care.'

Rebecca smiled kindly at Nicola and soothed her with a cuddle. Tears were streaming down the girl's face.

Downstairs the interview was concluding rather more cheerfully than it had begun, and Carlo made a parting concession. 'Sir James, I would not tell you how my debt came about, but I promise I will tell Nicola before we leave for Italy. She can make her decision then.'

After the confrontation in the study, Rebecca tried to lower the emotional temperature by giving Nicola a demonstration of the security system. Being involved in the art world had made her interested in such devices and she spoke knowledgeably for some minutes about the different types of sensors, cameras and other traps for the unwary burglar.

'There is a recording facility, too. Motion sensitive. Unless James overrides it, it comes on at six o'clock in the evening.'

'Is there a camera in every room?' asked Nicola, turning pale.

'No. Only ones where there might be something valuable. Kitchen, bathrooms, gym and so on are not on the circuit.'

'Oh,' said Nicola, relieved.

Rebecca eyed her closely. 'If you were working late in the study I expect you'd be on it,' she said with deliberate lightness.

'I suppose so,' said Nicola.

'Shall we look?' asked Rebecca, flicking through the file list of recordings on the computer.

'No, don't worry; I'm not very photogenic...' Nicola began hurriedly, but Rebecca had already pulled up the recording for the Monday when it had all begun.

'I think you're doing yourself an injustice, Nick. You look beautiful.'

Rebecca watched Nicola stare at the screen in confusion. The girl saw herself topless, bent over James' desk while he strapped her. They heard each crack of the leather and the cries which followed.

'You knew this was here, didn't you?' asked Nicola, realising that Rebecca had already watched the recording.

'Yes, but don't worry, Nick,' said Rebecca, 'you've been punished enough.'

'Silly of James not to erase it,' said Nicola. She sounded a little annoyed at his oversight.

'Yes, but it was only corroboration. I already knew: James breathless when I phoned from Italy;

ten o'clock at night and you were there; the lip-gloss and overnight bag on the Friday; and of course, *Fleurs de Paradis* on his clothes.'

Rebecca fast-forwarded the recording to the caning. 'He was a bit soft on you, I think,' she said, unimpressed by the moderate cuts whipping into the girl's backside.

'I suppose he was, compared to the caning he gave you,' said Nicola. 'Carlo wasn't soft on me, though.'

'No, that's true,' admitted Rebecca.

Suddenly they both jumped at the crack of the terrible sixth stroke. On screen Nicola swore and danced in pain.

'That one was a beauty, I'll give you that,' laughed Rebecca, and Nicola had to smile ruefully too.

'Actually I was so relieved he hadn't sacked me I would have taken sixty let alone six. It's not only the job; knowing James means having a little connection to Edward still.'

Nicola seemed about to cry again, so Rebecca gave her arm a squeeze. 'You're part of the family now.'

The answer to another riddle dawned on Nicola. 'Is this how you knew I'd watched you and James, that night?'

Rebecca smiled. 'Of course. It was a spectacular caning and I thought I'd see how I looked. I was being vain, I suppose. The camera caught you peering through the crack in the door.'

'What would James do if he knew we were here?' asked Nicola, out of the blue.

Rebecca gave her a withering look. 'I think we both know the answer to that.'

Nicola's question was oddly timed, because at that moment they turned to see James glaring at them from the door. He looked at the screen, where the closing stages of Monday's session were playing out.

'I noticed your car parked down the drive,' he said coldly to Rebecca, who was blushing.

Nicola tried to defuse the situation. 'James, I want to thank you for what you're doing, and for treating me like a... friend.' She hugged him warmly.

'Not at all,' he said distantly, locked in eye contact with Rebecca.

'I need to talk something over with Rebecca, Nick,' he continued, 'if you would excuse us. Call on Carlo. I think he has something to tell you.'

Alone with James Rebecca felt her temperature rise once more.

'I hoped Carlo would have been and gone before you returned,' he said at last.

'Evidently,' she replied, refusing to be apologetic.

'What I did with Nicola was wrong, so I'll not punish you for eavesdropping,' he said sternly.

'That's big of you,' she mocked. Her face was still hot with embarrassment at being caught. That was the way with men, she thought; they do something wrong but they make you feel guilty about it.

'I hope the portrait will go some way to making amends,' he said coolly.

They stared at each other in silence for a while. Really Rebecca would have liked him to bend her over the desk and lay into her with his belt. But all the passion was on her side; James seemed cold, almost offended.

'You know more of this business between Carlo and Nicola than you're letting on,' he said.

Stubbornly she refused to speak, but her blush deepened.

'It seems you're not prepared to be honest with me, even though you're soon to be my wife.'

His words stung her more than his cane ever had. She felt like following Nicola's example and crying, but instead she pushed past him. 'I have to go back to work,' she said.

Carlo spent most of his time now at Nicola's flat and Rebecca was alone at the cottage. She decided to watch some television and have an early night. Normally she would go to James', but his cold words had hurt her deeply. She brooded on the afternoon's events: the crisis with Nicola had been resolved, but somehow her engagement was still in jeopardy. Was this how married life would be? Would it always be her that had to apologise; he would always be right even when he'd done something wrong? She liked a strong hand, but she wanted it to be fair.

In bed she found solace in a favourite fantasy. It took place in a medieval castle, although the period was contemporary. In the banqueting hall four men sat around a long oak table. They all wore evening dress, but were of different ages and appearance.

Wearing only a PVC spanking skirt and high black stilettos, Rebecca waited on them. She had to keep her head lowered and never make eye contact with them. The tightness of the skirt and the height of the heels made her unsteady. She was conscious of her naked bottom exposed by the skirt. She ladled soup into a dish for the fat middle-aged man, but when he grabbed at her breast some spilled on the table. He pulled her across his lap and spanked her. Next she had to go round the table, being put across each man's lap in turn. Each spanking felt different. The hands of one were rough, those of a young labourer. Another's were strong but smooth, with long delicate fingers, like those of a pianist. The final man looked similar to James, but his hands were much larger; it was like being hit with a table tennis bat.

After dinner the men stayed at the table drinking brandy and smoking cigars. Rebecca had to stand on the table and sing to them. A small band accompanied her from the musician's gallery above. For this part of the fantasy she varied what she was wearing. Tonight she wore a figure-hugging evening dress in burgundy chiffon.

Each of the men had an implement next to him on the table: cane, flogger, tawse and paddle. The man with the cane rapped it against her calves. If her voice faltered she was made to get down and bend over each side of the table in turn, while the man from that side gave her twelve strokes with his implement. Each would choose whether or not to roll up her dress and pull down her knickers. The band would stop playing and the thwacks would reverberate around the hall. After the four beatings she had to climb back onto the table and sing again.

When the men had had enough of the singing they called for a footman, who roughly tore her dress from her. Then she had to dance on the table in her underwear. Since her heels were so high she danced mainly by swaying to the rhythm of the music, writhing her arms and hips as seductively as possible. When she stumbled she had to climb down again and take her beating on each side of the table. At the end of his twelve strokes each man would fuck her doggy style. Their hands were never gentle or caressing; they gripped and slapped her as though tenderising a piece of meat.

Sometimes her punishment would run into the next day, when she would be dragged naked into the stables. The four men, now dressed in country tweeds, would look on as the footman tied her to a post and thrashed her. Rebecca had never been properly whipped in real life and never wanted to be, but she was excited by the idea of it, knowing that four pairs of male eyes greedily devoured her plight, and that the men were aroused by her screams.

Although her fantasies always satisfied her, she would have much preferred the reality of being with James in his bed.

Chapter 11

Anxious to complete her painting as soon as possible, Carlo had pressed Rebecca to sit for him both days before Christmas. She and James wanted it to be set in his drawing room, in which was some lovely furniture, so she had to spend time at his house when her bitterness at James might otherwise have kept her away.

Carlo had made preliminary sketches on Tuesday evening. Rebecca bought sandwiches on the way from work so that she need not eat with James. He mostly kept to his study and left them in the drawing room alone. Now and again he had tried to smooth over the rift, but she'd not responded well. She sensed his new lack of trust in her, made all the more mortifying by her knowledge that it was justified.

On Christmas Eve Rebecca could spare the whole day because her office was closed, so Carlo began the painting proper. Fortunately the light was good during the morning and the pale sun shone into the room, bringing a gleam to her long brown hair.

Rebecca sat in a Thomas Sheraton armchair, leaning forward slightly, her hand resting over its arm. The chair was positioned side on, and her face was turned towards the painter. She was dressed in white, in a simple silk dress. She wore the pearls lent to Nicola for the ball.

At first her face held the trace of a smile that she did not feel, and Carlo soon asked her to lose it.

He worked quickly and in deep concentration. He said very little, so Rebecca was left to her own thoughts. Having already sat for one portrait in recent weeks she was bored by it all, and her pose was beginning to give her a stiff neck.

She thought most often about James and how fortunate she had been to land him. He had long been hunted as one of the English art world's most eligible singles. Among the cognoscenti the whisper was that his consorts could expect a spanking now and again, but that just made him a more exciting prospect to his admirers.

Of course Rebecca knew now that he was capable of more than a mere spanking, but that suited her down to the ground. She had disdained boyfriends who let her tantrums and extravagance go unchecked. Others had responded in the opposite way by dropping her as too much trouble.

Only James handled her well. With him Rebecca could sometimes exercise her wild side, be punished for it and move on; their relationship strengthened. In her professional life she needed to be self-controlled and commanding of others, so it was liberating that in her personal life someone else decreed how far she could go.

The house was particularly quiet, because James had gone to London for a meeting with Scotland Yard and the Crown Prosecution Service, who were deciding if a case could be brought against Francesco. He had given all the staff, including Nicola, a day's holiday, so Rebecca and Carlo had the place to themselves. James had said he would not be home until late as he expected the meeting to last all afternoon, and he intended to do some shopping afterwards. It would be an opportunity to buy Rebecca's Christmas present, he'd said, grinning, trying to lighten her mood. In response she gave him a stony look. Did he imagine, she wondered, that leaving her present to the last minute would somehow endear him to her? Men had strange ideas as to what pleased women.

By one-thirty Carlo had been working for nearly four hours. To Rebecca's relief he was beginning to tire. A tray of chicken sandwiches and a cold pork pie had been left for them in the kitchen, so she fetched them, together with a bottle of white wine from the cooler. Carlo opened the wine and they ate and drank in silence.

By now he had finished all the engagements the gallery had arranged for his trip. His contract was finalised and he would already have returned to Italy had it not been for this commission, and with no more work matters to discuss Rebecca found she did not have a lot to say to him. His magic had begun to pall and she would be glad when he was gone. His presence reminded her of her indiscretion, which she had come to regret. She would prefer to be free to criticise James' fling with Nicola without a guilty niggle of her own.

Now that the threat from the syndicate was gone the saturnine mood which had descended on Carlo at the ball had also lifted. His easy arrogance returned, and although charmed by it when first they met, Rebecca now found it juvenile and tedious. Since James had just saved his bacon she expected him to be a little more humble.

After lunch they carried on until three o'clock. As the light faded Carlo was attending to less important parts of the canvas, and he became more chatty. He spoke warmly of his feelings for Nicola, which Rebecca thought were genuine. This led him to reminisce about his first meeting with her at the cottage. It was something Rebecca did not want to talk about and she tried to discourage him, but to no avail. And when he began to insinuate that James would be displeased to learn who had engineered Nicola's trap, Rebecca began to get annoyed.

'It's water under the bridge, Carlo,' she said. 'Let's just forget about it.'

'Sir James has been good to me,' he persisted. 'Maybe it is my duty to tell him, especially when he is so concerned about Nicola's welfare.'

'Are you threatening me?' she asked heatedly.

'Of course not,' he said smoothly, 'but I wonder if we should come to some arrangement.'

'What arrangement?' she asked. James had been right about Carlo; he was despicable.

'We were too severe with her. I think we should make amends... or rather, you should.'

'What arrangement?' repeated Rebecca, through gritted teeth.

'I will punish you. For Nicola's sake, you understand.'

'For your sake you mean, you sadistic bastard!'

Carlo did not lose his temper. 'That wasn't what you called me in Milan,' he sneered.

'That was just holiday sex,' she said derisively,

'and I'll regret it for the rest of my life.'

'It seems now you have the contract you wish to discard me. Did you sleep with me to make me come to your gallery?'

'Don't be ridiculous, Carlo. In any case, you're with Nicola now.'

Carlo carefully carried the portrait out to the car. When he returned he began to pack up his easel and paints. Rebecca watched him bitterly, unable to understand how she once thought his slick movements graceful.

'James is the only person who should punish me,' she said at last.

'Perhaps, but he cannot punish you for sins he does not know,' he said, continuing to clear up. 'If you prefer that I told him, then of course he would be able to.'

The little shit had twisted her words back on her. 'No, I won't do it,' she declared.

'I'm sorry to hear that. I might also mention to Sir James about our little games in Milan.'

He had her in a corner and they both knew it. Rebecca's face was red with frustration. She couldn't see how to avoid consenting to Carlo's demands. Perhaps if she came clean to James before Carlo got to him, she thought. There was too much at stake. James might well feel so affronted that he would call off the engagement. Some of his views were rather old-fashioned. Although he thought it wrong for married men to have affairs, he thought it much worse for married women to do so. It came from his upbringing and she just had to accept it.

The sun had set and the room was becoming dark. Carlo was watching her patiently in the growing dusk without saying a word. He knew when to keep quiet.

'Very well,' she sighed. 'On one condition: if you try to have sex with me I'll tell Nicola.'

'As you wish.'

He took more kit out to the car, and when he returned he brought the wooden paddle and leather flogger.

'Without your dress, I think,' he told her. 'I wouldn't like to spoil its elegant lines.'

While Rebecca took off her dress Carlo dragged the Sheraton armchair into the centre of the room, and switched on the wall lights. With them the lights of the tall Christmas tree came on. She had decorated it for James in happier circumstances, taking far more care over it than she had with her own.

'What about my underwear?' she asked.

'Leave it on,' he replied, admiring her white stockings and suspenders, 'for the time being.'

He made her kneel on the leather seat of the chair and grip its arms for support.

'Hold on tightly, Rebecca,' he advised, and simultaneously delivering a whack of the paddle to her panty-clad behind.

As Carlo settled into his task his blows became crueller and Rebecca's gasps became squeals. Periodically he stopped to examine the pink skin beneath the white panties. He patted and prodded her rump and adjusted her position to his satisfaction, making sure knees and thighs were pressed together.

'Your bottom is a little larger than Nicola's,' he said gloatingly. 'It gives me a wider target.'

The paddling continued. On reaching twelve he lowered her panties to her knees. 'From now on you must count the strokes,' he ordered.

After the next punishing blow Rebecca gasped, 'Thirteen.'

Carlo was varying his aim; sometimes up and down each cheek and sometimes across both. He then delivered twelve hard strokes to the same spot on her right buttock, and a similar dozen to the left. It was agony, but Rebecca remembered how he had done the same to Nicola. At least some of Rebecca's guilt was assuaged by the beating being just as severe as the girl's had been. By now she was in so much pain that her position was slipping. Her knuckles were white gripping the arms of the chair, and she had just rested her forehead on its back when he told her to stand up and face him. Her panties fell to the floor, and he picked them up and used them to mop his brow.

'I have had to do all the work today, while you have been lounging in this chair,' he chuckled.

She said nothing but looked at him with disdain. Her jaw was set tight against the lingering pain in her rear. His smile was replaced by a determined look.

He ordered her to take off her bra. She let it fall to the floor. Carlo held the flat of the paddle under each breast in turn, lifting them gently. Skilfully he flicked her nipples without hurting them, and Rebecca was annoyed when they stiffened. He tried to cajole her into changing her mind about sex.

'In return I will make your punishment more bearable,' he goaded, but when she refused he made her bend over the chair again, this time with her legs spread wide, and she braced herself for more suffering.

The blows started at the top of each cheek and worked down to her stocking tops. Her breasts quivered with the impact of each stroke, and then he stopped again. She felt his fingers brushing her pubic hair.

'Don't you dare!' she snapped, and his response was to slap her buttocks and pinch their hot flesh until she cried out. Then he continued the paddling even harder than before.

At last the end came. 'Sixty!' she cried with relief. She was shaking but she refused Carlo's offer of support. Nor did she allow him to rub any lotion into her. She took the bottle from him and lay prone on the chaise longue, waiting for the stinging to subside. Then she reached behind and massaged some of the cream into the damaged areas.

A few minutes later the heat of the pain had eased, although her bottom felt bruised and tender. When she glanced up she saw Carlo stripped to the waist, smiling down at her.

'We should begin the second stage of your punishment,' he said.

'You can't flog me straight after the paddling!' exclaimed Rebecca. 'Nicola had days to recover.'

'True, but we haven't the time, have we?' he

shrugged.

'You must give me some time to rest.' She heaved herself up and went upstairs to lie down on James' bed, without recovering her bra and panties. No doubt they would only have to come off again later.

Apart from the physical anguish her heart was heavy from the quarrel with James and the nagging worry that Carlo may continue to be a threat to her marriage. His deal with her gallery would bring him to London quite often, and she suspected he'd have no scruples about blackmailing her again.

How she rued her hot-headed retribution against Nicola. Sow the wind and reap the whirlwind, she thought, as she fell into a recuperative doze.

When Rebecca awoke soon after five o'clock her heart sank as she recalled her new dilemma. Reluctantly she rose from the bed and examined her bottom in James' cheval mirror. She doubted that her sore skin could stand another beating so soon after being paddled. Even aside from the agony, the bruises would take an age to go. It was poor consolation that she was unlikely to sleep with James for a while, so that the marks would not matter.

Slowly she went downstairs. Carlo lounged on the drawing room sofa, idly sketching objects in the room.

'Are you feeling better, my sweet?' he asked solicitously.

She wanted to shout that she was not 'his sweet',

but she hadn't the energy. She didn't know whether her fighting spirit had been sapped by residual stupor from her nap or the misery of her predicament.

'How do you want me?' she asked listlessly.

'Naked apart from the shoes,' Carlo replied brightly. Even had his voice sounded less cheerful, his trousers confirmed how he revelled in her distress.

She looked for the chair to bend over, but it had been moved back to its original position.

'Where?' she asked, removing her stockings and suspender belt.

'Standing at the mantelpiece,' he said.

Dutifully she went over to it. A large carriage clock stood in the centre, which she moved along so she could rest her arms on the ledge. On the wall in front of her face was an enchanting eighteenth century landscape. She had forgotten who it was by and looked for the artist's signature.

Meanwhile Carlo was dictating the rules whose infraction would bring penalty strokes. Finally he told her to cheer up, because soon her suffering would be over.

'Since you are sad I will make a concession,' he added. 'You need not count the lashes.'

Quietly he came up behind her and pushed her hair over her shoulder, away from her back.

'Keep your shoulders clear, ready for any extras,' he said, letting the tails of the flogger play over her flesh.

She had not wanted to give him the satisfaction of screaming, but after the first few lashes she could not help herself. She twisted her head in pain and her hair fell back over her shoulders.

'One extra for moving the position of your hair,' he said gleefully.

Rebecca was confused. Had there been such a rule that she'd missed? It seemed so mean. But then that was probably what he intended it to be. She smoothed her hair back in front and immediately her shoulders flinched as the penalty lash struck them. Rebecca tried to take her mind off the pain by studying the picture a few inches from her eyes.

After another two strokes there was a further penalty for throwing back her hair. To avoid it happening again Carlo allowed her to change her stance. He told her to take a step back from the mantelpiece, bend forward from the waist and support herself by resting her hands rather than her forearms on it. With her arms straightened in this way she could lower her head and let her hair fall forward, leaving her back uncovered.

Rebecca had lost count of the number he'd given her across her buttocks, but guessed it was about ten. Another thirty seemed impossible to bear. She wondered whether she would faint as Nicola had done.

She steeled herself for the next lash, but it never came. Instead she heard a thud and turned in astonishment to see Carlo on the floor with James standing over him.

'James!' she cried, but her heart sank when she saw the look of fury on his face.

On the whole Carlo looked like a man who

could handle himself, but he was plainly reluctant to fight back against his generous benefactor. Perhaps he also recognised that being caught tampering with another man's naked fiancée deserved a punch. In any case he scrambled to his feet, and when James told him to get out he did not dawdle.

Rebecca and James stared at each other, and her earlier resentment flared up again. 'You're always sneaking up on me!' she cried.

'Sneaking up?' He sounded flabbergasted. 'If you weren't behaving deceitfully my movements around my own house wouldn't seem like sneaking up!'

Rebecca began to dress gingerly. 'It's not what you think,' she said.

'How can it be otherwise?' he said icily. 'You're sleeping with him.'

'No!' she denied, and then looked him steadily in the eye. 'Once,' she admitted quietly. 'In Milan. It was a mistake.'

He glared back at her but said nothing. His silence goaded her.

'You slept with Nicola,' she said accusingly, and at least he was shamefaced enough to lower his eyes.

'How can we go on with this lack of trust between us,' he asked, more in sorrow than in anger.

Rebecca groaned. It all seemed so unfair. For the second time in a few days she felt close to tears. Feeling wounded and humiliated she slipped off her engagement ring and handed it to him.

There was a flicker in his eyes, but he accepted it without speaking, so she left.

Rebecca and Carlo had come in the same car, and at least the bastard had waited for her. She got in without looking at him and sat in silence as he drove away.

At the cottage they found Nicola waiting outside. When Carlo had not turned up at her flat or answered her calls, she decided to come over to see him. She took in his black eye and Rebecca's distressed state with astonishment. He slunk off in shame to the pub, leaving Nicola to help Rebecca inside and make her a hot toddy.

Over the course of the next hour Rebecca related the horrors of the day. She did so in fragments, between periods of feeling so utterly desolate that she could not speak. Nicola was caring and compassionate. At the end Rebecca broke down, her tears, so long held back, flowing. She apologised for being such a baby, worried her crying might diminish the girl's respect for her.

'It's okay,' whispered Nicola, holding Rebecca's head to her shoulder. 'We're girls. We're allowed to cry.'

Nicola was so upset with Carlo that she did not want him to come back to her flat, but realised it would be quite wrong to let him stay at the cottage alone with Rebecca.

After they had gone Rebecca rose listlessly and put on a favourite CD. She was indulging her grief too much, she told herself. 'Snap out of it,' her father would have said, but somehow she couldn't.

The second track was Handel's aria, *Lascia ch'io pianga*; Almirena lamenting her separation from her knight. At least she was reunited with him in the end. Rebecca had lost hers for good. *Let me weep*.

She curled up on the sofa, recalling times spent with James and cursing the day she ever met Carlo.

She was awoken by the sound of church bells. After brooding for hours she must have drifted off to sleep. It was Christmas Eve and people would be going to Midnight Communion. Rebecca was not a very religious person, but she decided to join them, hoping it might divert her from self pity.

St Mary's was less than five minutes' walk from her cottage. It was the largest church of the local villages, so it tended to be the one used for special occasions. She passed the pub, which had a late license, and sounds of drunken revelry came from inside. Smokers hunched shivering and chatting around the doorway. Cars were everywhere, spilling out of the pub's small car park, around the village green and along the lane by the church. The noise from the pub receded as the bells grew louder. Rebecca joined a steady stream of people making their way up the path to the porch.

One or two people she knew slightly wished her good evening and she responded with a thin smile. She realised her mood must have seemed to them rather lacking in festive cheer. She was struck by the way many of them knew each other and gathered together in cheerful groups. Spending a lot of time in Oxford and London she had never really been drawn into village life. Secretly she tended to look down on it as boring and petty in comparison with her own career, but she realised that many people drew fulfilment from it simplicity.

The church was nearly full. Rebecca slipped into a pew near the back. Although those around her sang the opening hymn with gusto she sang quietly, looking about her at the architecture: slender grey stone pillars and gothic arches. The tower and nave dated from the early fourteenth century. A small Lady Chapel was even older. With a twinge of sadness she recalled walking around it with James one quiet Saturday, admiring the intricate stone carving.

Caught up in the prayers she found some solace and forgot her troubles for a while, but during the sermon her mind began to drift back to them. Predictably the vicar was speaking of Mary and motherhood, and Rebecca wondered if she would ever have children. She wondered if, in time, she would find another man to love as much as she did James. At the moment it seemed doubtful.

People had been bringing their sorrows within these walls for nearly seven centuries, and she was sure that matters of unrequited love had figured prominently in their prayers. Perhaps some were answered, but she thought it probable that most were not; that seemed to be the nature of the human lot. But just in case she said a silent prayer for her cousin Mark's family. It was strange how sadness of your own brought other people's tragedies to mind.

The hard pew began to hurt and it was a relief to kneel for The Creed. Rebecca wasn't sure she believed the words, but they were phrased to sound soothing when spoken. She hesitated over whether or not to take communion, but in the end she did, carried along by the people from her pew. She sipped the wine and swallowed the tasteless wafer, then returned to her seat as inconspicuously as possible.

As she left the church a clean-cut man in a navy cashmere coat and silk scarf wished her a happy Christmas. He was an accountant whom she knew slightly, a partner with a medium sized firm in Oxford. Normally she found money men rather soulless, but he had nice eyes which were looking sympathetically into hers. He knew she'd been crying, she sensed.

It transpired that he was recently divorced, so maybe he was angling for a date. She knew she would be in no condition to see somebody new for a while, but she smiled at him and left the door open. He had his hand in the small of her back, gently guiding her past groups of people, and as she turned to go he lowered it and firmly patted her bottom. In the crowd it was difficult to tell for sure whether it was intentional, but it was interesting.

After a good night's sleep she drove down to Hampshire to spend the holiday with her parents.

Chapter 12

James spent a bleak Christmas, mainly alone. On New Year's Eve he went to a party in London. He enjoyed catching up with friends, but he had to endure endless sympathy when he told them about his break up. On the whole he was glad when the holidays were over and normality returned. His only reservation was that the first full week in January would be Nicola's last. He smiled ruefully when he remembered that, just a month ago, he had wanted to sack her.

Feeling sorry for himself he had half planned to try to dissuade her from moving to Italy, and perhaps even ask her to be his girlfriend. But saner thoughts had prevailed; the age difference was too great, and although they were fond of each other it was not, he suspected, enough for either of them. Moreover, dreadful though Carlo was, she claimed to love him, and James saw that he could help Nicola best by trying to take on aspects of Edward's role, so that the girl was not adrift in the world without family.

When Friday came he ineptly put these thoughts to her. He emphasised that he had meant her to take seriously what she'd overheard him telling Carlo. He didn't use the word 'daughter' to her face because it didn't seem appropriate after their sexual encounters, but instead he said he would help to protect her interests whenever she felt she needed him. Nicola blushed nicely and pecked him on the cheek. She seemed grateful.

At lunchtime she surprised him by returning early, and came into the study just as he was cradling a diamond choker in his hands.

'Whoa!' she exclaimed. 'Lucky girl who gets that!'

James was worried that she might think it was a leaving gift for her. 'It was Rebecca's Christmas present,' he explained hurriedly. 'I noticed her admiring it a couple of months ago. She never guessed I would buy it because it was so expensive, but I went back and bought it the same day.'

'Oh,' murmured Nicola, 'so that was the last minute present.'

James looked up sharply. It never failed to amaze him, the details women would share with each other. 'I was just teasing her when I said that.'

'It's very beautiful,' she said, gazing in wonder at the quantity of diamonds. 'It must have cost the earth.'

'Well, the price of a small island, anyway,' he said wryly.

He put the choker back in its case. Rebecca's engagement ring was next to it on the desk and he slipped both of them into his desk drawer.

'Did you want me, Nicola?' he asked, his manner becoming businesslike.

'Actually, James, I wanted to ask you a favour.'

Nicola explained that she intended to let her flat furnished, but that she had some furniture of sentimental value which she didn't want to leave there. So she asked him to store it for her while she was in Italy, which he readily agreed to do.

But this wasn't enough for Nicola; she wanted him to come to see the furniture to make sure he was happy with the space it would take up. Given the vastness of James' house this seemed to him pointless, but he humoured her. It would be a convenient way of saying goodbye on her last day without too much emotion.

They each took their own car, since Nicola would not be returning. She packed up her personal belongings, and he was in his car ready to follow her when she had to dash back for something she'd forgotten. Some red lingerie peeped out of the bag she brought out and with mixed emotions he remembered the afternoon she'd worn it.

He smiled when she blew a kiss to the house and waved it goodbye.

At home Nicola seemed to have become more tense. James supposed it was due to the impending goodbye or the excitement of soon starting her new life.

The living room was much emptier than on his previous visit. Rectangular patches on the walls showed where pictures had hung. All plants and ornaments had disappeared. One or two cardboard boxes stood waiting to be taken to some place of storage, and he noticed their suitcases already packed in the hall.

'You've tidied up at last.' It was a feeble joke, but she laughed.

Mercifully Carlo was not in evidence. Nicola had told James that Rebecca had kicked him out of her cottage, and James had not looked forward to the awkwardness of meeting him at Nicola's.

She pressed him to have a drink and he accepted a small scotch. They talked a little about her plans in Milan. There was no job yet but she hoped to get one soon, and Rebecca had promised to speak to her contacts in the art galleries there.

Then abruptly she changed the subject.

'James, don't get all huffy on me, but there's something I want to tell you.'

He bristled a bit to find that she thought he could be huffy, but when she started to talk about his relationship with Rebecca he realised that huffy was what he felt. It embarrassed him to talk openly about his private life.

'Carlo forced Rebecca to take that beating on Christmas Eve,' she told him.

'How could he force her?' he asked frostily.

'He threatened to tell you that they'd had sex when she sat for him in Milan.'

'So her response was to have sex with him again?' he said sceptically.

'No. He wanted sex but she refused. She only accepted the punishment.'

'How do you know this?'

'Rebecca told me,' said Nicola. When she added that she had prised the same story out of Carlo James accepted it grudgingly.

'So how can you put yourself in the hands of this man?' he asked incredulously.

'For the time being I love him and I can live with his flaws. But we were talking about Rebecca and you,' she continued. 'Carlo also blackmailed her with something else.'

She told him how Rebecca had conspired with Carlo to punish her for seducing James. She told him about the paddling and the whipping at the cottage.

'You didn't seduce me,' he objected, 'it was my doing.'

She waved the quibble aside. 'The point is that Rebecca thought I was trying to steal you from her.'

'I see.'

'She loved you so much she didn't want to lose you, and...' she paused, '...well, you know how mad she can get.'

'Why couldn't she confess all this to me herself?'

'It's too late now, and before she was too worried that you cared for me so much you might turn against her.'

'That doesn't seem likely. She knew I'd dealt with you pretty severely myself.'

They sat in silence, and glumly he mulled over this new information. No one had come out of the events of the last month with much credit, he thought, but perhaps Rebecca's conduct now appeared a little less culpable.

'I just wanted you to know,' said Nicola. 'In case it made a difference.'

'Well, where's this furniture I need to look at?' he sighed, bringing the discussion to an end. He put his glass on the coffee table and stood up.

Nicola's flat had three bedrooms. She led him to one of them and unlocked the door.

Must be valuable if she keeps it locked up, he

thought, but once inside he realised the true reason for the security.

Nicola switched on the wall lamps. The room's brocade curtains were clearly kept drawn. In the centre of the floor was an odd piece of wooden furniture, a whipping bench. He could well understand that she would not want to leave it for the tenants. Its shape recalled a vaulting horse, but it was smaller and plusher. The dark oak sides tapered from the base to a narrow top of padded leather. The wood shone as though recently polished. Leather restraints with brass buckles were attached to its sides at various points.

Apart from the bench the only furniture in the room was a Victorian cabinet, a straight-backed chair and an old-fashioned cheval mirror, similar to the one in James' own bedroom. Nicola told him they had all stood in her punishment room at Edward's house. Although this room was smaller, she had tried to replicate the decoration and layout of the original as closely as possible. They stood for a moment, absorbing the atmosphere. Despite being kept locked the room was well aired and warm.

Nicola became more confiding. Sometimes, she said, she would come into the room and lie across the bench and fantasise about Edward or James finding her there.

'And then what happens?' he asked, flattered that he should appear in her fantasy.

'You can guess when you look in the cupboard,' she said, then showed him the contents. He picked up some of the items to examine them. One was a narrow and gnarled school cane with the traditional crook handle.

While he looked Nicola sat shyly on the chair.

'Apart from me, you're the only person to come in this room,' she said. 'I always hoped to find someone worthy to bring here, but I never did.'

'What about Carlo?' he asked.

'It was going to be his Christmas present, but he spoiled that on Christmas Eve.'

'Well I can arrange for the bench and cabinet to be taken to my place discreetly,' he said briskly, but she ignored his comment.

'How would you like me?' she whispered, looking up at him with bright eyes.

'I beg your pardon?'

'We had a deal. That Friday, my last punishment session was interrupted. Before I leave I want to pay my debt.'

She had a wicked way of arousing him with a word and a look. He gazed at her hungrily for a few moments, drinking in her submissive beauty.

He nodded. 'Very well,' he agreed, 'but who said you may sit down, young lady?'

She got to her feet immediately and said, 'I'm sorry, sir.'

'An extra stroke of the cane,' he said.

'Yes, sir. How would you like me, sir?' she repeated. 'There are some uniforms in the cabinet.'

He thought for a moment, and then replied, 'I want you... pure and simple.'

'I'm sorry, sir?' she queried, not understanding.

'I want you completely naked,' he clarified.

She laughed and said, 'But, as sir knows I am

not so pure.'

'I'll see what I can do to correct that over the next hour or so,' he promised.

As she hung her clothes in the cabinet Nicola slipped out of her role for a moment. 'Could I ask you to do something, James?' she asked timidly. 'Would you be naked too?'

'But what about Carlo?' he asked.

'I promised him we wouldn't have sex,' she said.

James was confused. 'Promised him?' he echoed.

'I told him this would happen today. I explained about my deal with you. After what he did to Rebecca he couldn't complain.'

'I see,' he said. 'Where is Carlo, by the way?' The last thing James wanted was for Carlo to be waiting in the sitting room while he was punishing Nicola.

'He's agreed to do the tourist thing in Oxford and spend the night in a hotel there.' James was pleased Nicola was standing up to Carlo. He believed him to be the sort of man who would run roughshod over people if they gave in to him.

'His New Year's resolution is never to have sex with anyone else while he's with me,' she went on, 'so I have to abide by that too.'

'I understand,' said James as he undressed. 'I think a bit more faithfulness would be good for us all after the last few weeks.

'Now, I seem to recall that you've already had the hand-spanking. What remains are the strap and the cane. Can you remember how many strokes you were to have?'

'Twelve of the strap and eighteen of the cane,'

she replied promptly.

'Correct,' he said. 'However, since my preferred implements are not here I will choose two from your collection. And in order to make my choice I need a bottom to test them on, Nicola.'

He made her kneel on the bench, head low and bottom in the air. Seeing the beautiful target made him regret telling her there would be no spanking, and he couldn't resist reaching out to feel the stretched silkiness of the twin globes.

The cupboard contained straps, canes and birch rods. There was three of each. He followed the same procedure with each implement; taking it from the cupboard, swishing it twice through the air, then delivering one moderate stroke across the middle of Nicola's bottom. The straps were solid and heavy, but rather cumbersome to wield, so he reserved judgment on them.

Before moving on to the canes he examined her bottom. The lovely white flesh had become pink, but showed no marks.

The canes were good; long and whippy with a satisfying swish. The last of the three produced a shudder and a yelp from her.

'I think I've found my first implement,' he decided.

She groaned, suspecting his second would be a birch. And she was right. In the end he selected the second of the rods he'd used. It was a little over three feet long with four supple branches bound by a red leather handle. It had also elicited a yelp from Nicola.

As planned he told her he would use a cane for

eighteen strokes, plus the extra one already earned. For the twelve strokes the original strap would be replaced by the birch. The birching would follow the caning. He made her stand up straight facing the mirror to listen to the rules about posture, counting and swearing. As he lectured her she watched him in the mirror and giggled at the excited condition of his erection. Being naked together with no prospect of sex felt strange, but intensely erotic.

He then delivered the first six strokes of the caning with Nicola bent over the chair. He made her stand on tiptoe, legs together. After each stroke he allowed her to come down from her toes while he ran his fingers along the new stripe left on her skin. He didn't hold back, annoyed when she'd told him Edward's strokes were harder than his. He felt she had been let of lightly the first time, and besides, he was no longer worried about her ability to withstand punishment as he had been, as he knew now how cruelly Carlo had treated her.

Nicola bravely submitted to the session, though she no longer had a need to. If she sought to fulfil her agreement because she found him a soft touch next to Edward and Carlo, he would make her regret it. James was determined to give her a beating to remember him by. After all, what she had done warranted it, especially the calculated nature of her errors.

The first six were taken well and Nicola counted the strokes clearly. She remained bent over the chair with her legs and bottom quivering a little from her tiptoe stance, waiting for the seventh. He made her hold the difficult posture for a minute or so while he watched her. Then he had her kneel on the seat of the chair and lean over its back.

The caning was about to become more severe. He wanted to hear her cry out so he knew he was getting through to her. And cry out she did, with ever louder wails as the cane cut into her cheeks.

On the twelfth stroke the cane cracked in the middle. Nicola jumped off the chair, howling in agony and holding her bottom. Another extra was chalked up. After calming down she resumed her kneeling position on the chair.

He let her stay there for a moment, her face screwed up in pain and tears flowing while he selected a replacement cane. Then he took her by the arm and led her to the bench. He made her mount astride it and lie forward. There were cuffs conveniently placed to hold her wrists and ankles, but he did not restrain her. Her arms and legs simply hung loose and she rested her cheek on the padded leather, gazing at him with wet eyes.

'You asked for a severe beating, young lady,' he said sternly.

'Yes, sir,' she whimpered.

'There are six of the original cane strokes remaining, plus two extras. Are you sure you want me to continue?'

'Yes, sir, I'm sure.'

They were delivered alternately to each buttock. At first she would flinch as she watched his arm fall, so he had her turn her face away from him.

The penultimate stroke swept against her left

cheek. It was a ferocious cut forcing a scream from the girl, but nevertheless when she bucked and snatched her hands to her bottom he told her she would have another penalty stroke. She took time to recover before counting it, and there were now two remaining, which he delivered harshly to her right buttock.

She shuddered and screamed, before mumbling, 'Twenty-one, sir.'

By this time her bottom was a mass of red flesh crisscrossed with fierce welts. He rested the cane across the small of her back and sat on the seat, watching her. The cane rose and fell with her shuddering sobs, until the worst of the pain had passed and her breathing became more normal.

Eventually he rose and walked around the bench, studying the damage inflicted. He was concerned that the birching on top of it might be too much, but Nicola had proved herself to be highly resilient, and he decided to proceed as planned.

He mentioned that he had not seen any lotion in the cupboard, and she told him where to find some in the bathroom. When he returned she was still over the bench, but her right hand was beneath her gently moving body and he could hear her faint sighs of pleasure. Clearly she was feeling much better.

'What are you doing?' he asked sternly, slapping her buttocks.

'Please sir, may I relieve myself?' she begged meekly.

'I thought there was to be no sex.'

'I meant with each other,' she replied. 'Would you like to masturbate too, sir?'

He would have loved to do so, and now he had parted from Rebecca no moral ties prevented him, but he did not deem it fitting in his putative role as Nicola's protector. However, he didn't prevent her from continuing to masturbate as he gently rubbed cream into her bottom. It took immense self-restraint on his part not to touch his cock, which was throbbing enticingly. Nicola savoured a shuddering little orgasm, and let her arm drape back down the side of the bench.

'You'll have an extra stroke of the birch for inappropriate behaviour,' he told her.

'Yes, sir. Thank you very much, sir.'

'Are you ready for worse to come, young lady?'

'Yes, sir.'

'Good.' Rather ominously James took her wrists and fastened them into the cuffs low down on the bench, and then he strapped her ankles and thighs with leather bands also fitted to it. He adjusted the buckles so her legs were held tightly together, then finally a belt which hung from one side of the bench top was drawn tightly over her waist and fastened into its buckle on the opposite side.

Nicola was so tightly squeezed into the bench that she could hardly move an inch. James had once asked a girl why she was so exhilarated by his beatings, and she replied that it excited her to be defenceless and at his mercy. This was certainly true of Nicola now. She could not struggle no matter what he chose to do to her.

She watched him intently as he picked up the

chosen birch rod. His erection was strong again but it brought no laughter from her now. He ran the firm twigs through his fingers. He knew it was lighter than the birches that had once been used for judicial floggings, but it was still more than enough for a young woman's delicate backside.

'How many strokes is it, young lady?' he asked her.

She was uncertain. 'Twelve... no, thirteen, sir,' she said with a query in her voice.

'Correct.'

'I've never had so many with the birch before,' she said in trepidation. 'Eight was the most Edward ever gave me.'

'I'm glad to know I'm improving on Edward at last,' he said, running the tips of the birch over her vulnerable back, bottom and thighs. As they tapped and tickled her she squirmed reflexively in her bonds.

'This will be painful,' he told her, her breathing heavy in anticipation.

His first stroke was of medium strength to test her reactions, but she still squealed. He waited, but nothing came.

'Count! I will not warn you again,' he threatened, then reminded her that although he would allow her ample recovery time, if she had not counted the previous stroke before he tapped her bottom in preparation for the next, she would earn an extra.

'I'm sorry, sir. One, sir.'

As he whipped the succeeding strokes across her bottom Nicola began to scream and sob. Each cut of the birch was equivalent to several concurrent strokes of the cane and Nicola was clearly suffering dreadfully. The restraints creaked as she jerked impotently against them. Lines and scratches quickly appeared on her buttocks, over the existing weals of the cane.

After the sixth stroke he rested the birch across her back and held her burning cheeks in his hands while the girl wept.

When he took up the rod again he played it over the soft skin at the top of her thighs. He covered the areas between the bottom of her cheeks and the leather band holding her thighs. She moaned, knowing what was coming.

The second half of the birching brought wilder screams from Nicola than before. He hoped the occupants of the flat above were at work, or the police may well be called. The tops of her legs and her full buttocks were blotchy and swollen with welts.

With two strokes left he wondered whether he should take pity on her and end it there. Her whines were continuous, her tears soaked into the leather pad.

He hesitated. Then he remembered how she had deliberately lost him twenty thousand pounds and his resolve hardened again. He delivered the penultimate stroke, to the crown of her bottom. He watched her writhe ineffectually in her tight bonds; at least they prevented penalties for losing position.

There was a long wait, but no count of the stroke. He left it two minutes, and then three. Her shrieks had subsided to a whimper. He glanced at his watch yet again. Five minutes had passed. He tapped her bottom and told her she would receive an extra. She sobbed in response.

He wanted to make sure she would not miscount the next stroke and prolong her ordeal, so he asked, 'What number's next?'

She had to think a moment before replying. 'Twelve, sir.'

'Correct. Remember to count it.'

Twelve fell as hard as its predecessors, cutting across existing stripes. Her screams were vehement, but eventually she managed to count through her sobs. The two penalties followed it and the fourteen strokes were complete.

At last Nicola's debt had been paid in full. He wondered whether she would have begged so eagerly for her punishment on that first Monday if she'd been able to see herself now, wracked by exhaustion and suffering.

Nicola asked James to stay with her that night, and he was happy to. She lay on her side, her bottom backed tantalisingly into his lap. He draped an arm over her and kissed her from time to time.

When she fell asleep he lay back, thinking about the unforeseen outcome of the day. The intensity of the experience had been exacerbated by there being no chance of sexual release.

He rose early the next morning, wanting to leave before Carlo returned. When he came back from the bathroom she was awake, and watched him dress.

'I'm impressed with your self-control, James,' she said. 'Most men would get into a right sulk if I didn't feel like sex when they did.'

'Well maybe I would, if I were *your* man,' he replied. Then after an affection kiss, he left.

At home later that morning James remembered he'd hurried off to Nicola's without locking the diamond choker in the safe, and when he opened his desk drawer he was dismayed to find that both it and the engagement ring had gone. He knew there had been no burglary and he trusted his domestic staff absolutely, so the unwelcome conclusion was that Nicola had taken them. Mischievous though she could be in matters of sex, she had always been utterly honest as an employee, so he simply could not believe she would steal from him.

'Unless,' he said aloud, 'that damned Carlo has put her up to it.'

When he called her home her answerphone cut in. He left a message, phrasing his words carefully, without implying guilt on her behalf. No return call came, and he spent an uncomfortable afternoon waiting in hope for one. In the evening he drove to her flat, but there was no response to the doorbell and everything was in darkness.

Back in his study his hand rested indecisively on the phone. He was inclined to call the police.

Chapter 13

Knowing what was kept in the boss' desk drawer only intensified Maria's feeling of being a little girl summoned before the headmaster. His dreary office was made more so by memories of that unpleasant night in December. A champion wrestler in his youth, the boss was more like a gorilla than any man she had ever seen. She stood before his desk and awaited her sentence.

When he told her that she was to be freed at last, her heart soared and the gloomy atmosphere was forgotten. Business had made the boss a ruthless and cynical man, but the better natured girls brought out a soft spot in him. He enfolded her in a farewell embrace. She was awed by his latent power, knowing that in his past these arms had crushed the breath from strong men. His warm wishes brought tears to her eyes, which embarrassed him, and he took refuge in irony.

'I nearly forgot; it seems I've become your social secretary,' he said, passing her a piece of paper with a name and phone number on it. Normally liaisons with the customers were forbidden, but he gave a shrug of his shoulders as if to say, *but since you're leaving...*

'He wanted your number,' he told her.

'Did you give it to him?' she asked.

'No. I told him this wasn't a dating agency.'

The message had been from Filippo, and she smiled to herself when she compared the brusque handling he would have had from the boss with

Bruno's toadying.

At the end of the interview he returned her passport, something she had not seen for two years. She really did cry then, so he gave her another hug. It was like being comforted by King Kong.

'Sometimes it is a hard lesson for girls to discover which men are good and which are evil,' he said gruffly.

He released her and gave the piece of paper in her hand a tap with a forefinger the size of a Cuban cigar. 'This one, I hear, is not too bad,' he said.

Maria packed her things and said goodbye to those colleagues already at work. Many of them had not yet arrived, because the club did not open for another two hours, but she didn't want to stay any longer than she had to.

Bruno was there of course, and Maria waved goodbye to him, prepared to let bygones be bygones. But the floor manager hated her for escaping his clutches and his response was dismissive. In the last few days he had turned his attentions to a pretty Asian waitress who had shown excitement when women were tied up on stage, and Maria suspected it would not be long before the girl found herself part of the show. She just hoped for her sake that the beatings would be as welcome as the bondage.

At first Maria was reluctant to return Filippo's call. For one thing she was leaving the country soon, so she thought that a relationship couldn't go anywhere. But more importantly her tribulations had taught her to be wary of men.

On the other hand, she knew the boss' restrained praise had actually been a glowing testimonial of Filippo. And she was elated by her new freedom: she was a nineteen year old who had not been on a proper date for two years, so it was time to live the normal life of a pretty girl again.

Filippo sounded delighted to hear from her. He apologised, time and time again, for the strapping, claiming it would never have happened if he had not been drunk. With her hard earned wisdom about the male sex Maria took his claims with a pinch of salt. She knew that a man who went to *La Pera* in the first place probably took pleasure in punishing women, but even so, she accepted a date for dinner the next evening.

They went to a good but homely restaurant. She felt comfortable and relaxed. It was a change for her not to have to please her companion and hang on his every word. She liked being able to talk about herself, but she was guarded: Filippo knew that she had worked in a sex club, but he did not know about the brothel. That would come out in time... if there was to be a time for the two of them.

Filippo treated her courteously and didn't assume that her old job made her an easy lay. If anything, the memory of their first meeting seemed to make him reluctant to touch her at all. On her doorstep she almost had to make the first move, before he sprung to life and kissed her, tentatively at first and then with increasing enthusiasm.

When his hand rested on her bottom he must have sensed her blush, because he backed off immediately.

'I'm sorry,' he said, 'I know the bottom is out of bounds.'

She laughed. 'It's not completely out of bounds, Filippo. We'll just have to agree access rights.'

He kissed her fervently again before they said goodnight.

That night *La Pera* had two very important guests. The gorilla himself showed them to their table, which was secluded but close to the action. Even he treated them with high deference, since they were, through a complex network of companies, the club's owners.

The elder of the two was a fat man who plumped into his place with a sigh. He let his ample body spread over the plush banquette seating which formed a horseshoe around the table. His lean companion was a much better advertisement for the renowned quality of their tailor. Both wore gold watches of a similar style, but otherwise their only jewellery was plain gold wedding rings. The fat man had obviously been married for many years, because his ring cut deep into his podgy finger.

As the boss left he paused by the next table, towering above the four mere giants who sat there. He shared a relaxed laugh with them. Twenty years previously he had sat at the same table doing the same job; a bodyguard to the two brothers.

When the brothers put their grey heads together

to discuss important business it was in total privacy, but minor matters were often ironed out in their leisure time. Tonight they wanted to draw a line under the case of Carlo's forgeries.

'How is Francesco?' asked the fat brother.

'Happy. There was not enough evidence to prosecute him.'

'He has lost the business though?'

'Yes, but the property lease alone is worth a few million. He wants to retire. He'll work as a consultant now and then, if we need him.'

A drum roll announced the prelude to the floor show. It was to be a special performance tonight and the club was full. Although countless girls were available to take part in the less demanding activities on stage, it was much harder to find suitable candidates for the main event. As *La Pera* was a legitimate business their consent was necessary, and they often chose to retire after only one or two appearances. Those that carried on needed several weeks to recover after each one. Consequently, many shows tended to be too tame for the strictest aficionados of pain. If on a given night the sternest treatment was to be meted out, usually only one girl would face it. Tonight however three girls were to be, metaphorically, sacrificed in honour of the pagan New Year, but fortunately the expansion of the EU had generated a flow of women from Eastern Europe to replenish the club's pool of submissive beauties.

The trio appeared on stage dressed in the tunics of slave girls in ancient Rome. Two of the girls were white and one was black. The show master appeared, dressed as a Roman centurion and ripped the tunic harshly off each girl, making her stagger. Naked, the girls stood facing the audience as the centurion walked around them. He examined their bodies, prodding and squeezing whichever parts took his fancy. On his command the girls turned their backs to the audience. He manhandled their buttocks in turn, to appreciative murmurs from the onlookers. Then the girls put their arms on each others' shoulders and circled in the manner of Canova's Three Graces, showing off their backs and bottoms. The curtain fell and the club's small band resumed their repertoire.

The fat man signalled to their waitress and gave her instructions. Then he turned back to his brother.

'Does Sir James know about us?' he asked.

'No I don't think so. Carlo would be afraid to tell him.'

'He might tell him, if he were threatened with the police.'

The thin man laughed sardonically. 'He is more afraid of us than of the police.'

'You think he helped Carlo just because of the girl?'

'I'm sure of it. She was his secretary and he had an affair with her.'

'And now she is coming to Italy. An opportune move.'

Whilst it had been a nuisance that James had spotted the first forgery, it seemed that he had withheld information about the second from the police. All in all the brothers did not feel he was a danger to them. Both believed in the maxim *he who does not help my enemy helps me*. They considered whether this soft spot in James' character might be of use to them in the future. Nothing sprang to their minds at the moment, but they had built long and successful careers by manipulating important men.

'It does no harm to have Sir James in reserve,' the younger man mused.

'Can she speak Italian?' asked the fat one, returning to the subject of Nicola.

'A little. Her father was a classics professor, I think.'

'Will she need a job here? We could suggest one to Carlo.'

'I'll speak to him. Something very upright and honest for the time being, I think.'

'Exactly.'

The black girl from the stage had been standing silently at their table waiting for the conversation to end. When the fat man turned to her she said, 'My Master told me you wish to inspect my bottom, signore.'

The fat man pushed the table away to make room for the girl to lie across his lap. He delicately patted her generous rump. Meanwhile the other made a phone call to his wife, paying no attention whatever to his brother and the girl.

'I would like to inspect you again later. At my town flat.'

'Certainly, signore.'

'Tell your Master to be merciful in the performance.'

'Yes, signore. Would you like him to accompany me to your flat?'

The fat man smiled. 'No. I think I can handle you alone. Reassure him that I intend to be very strict with you.'

'Of course, signore.'

'My driver will collect you from the dressing room after the show. Be ready for him,' he said, waving her away.

Now that the black girl had been dismissed the show could begin. The curtain rose on a stage with three identical pillories standing side by side. The centurion led in the naked slaves. Around the neck of each of them was a loop of string, from which hung a thin wooden rod. They stood, one in front of each pillory, heads humbly bowed, facing the audience. Each one took a pace forward as the centurion read out her name and crime from a parchment. Vibia, the black girl, was guilty of stealing a pear. Gaia and Lucia had been caught making love to each other. Gaia was petite, with small firm breasts and a boyish haircut. Her partner in crime had a fuller figure and long blonde hair.

The centurion took each girl to her pillory and locked her head and hands in it. The rods hung freely from their necks. The pillories were barely above waist height, so that the girls had to bend over whilst in them. A post jutted horizontally from each one, along which the girl could rest her upper body to hold her position. The two white girls were set with their bottoms to the audience, and the black girl between them, facing the audience.

The centurion was heavily built with huge hands, which he used to deliver a hard spanking to each slave. His hand seemed to cover the entire surface of one of Gaia's slender buttocks. As each smack landed the girl's body jerked, causing her rod to swing like a pendulum. All the girls were experienced and received their spanks in silence, knowing to save their breath for later.

The centurion lifted the rod off each girl in turn, wound the string loop round the end to thicken his grip, and delivered six slashing strokes to her backside. After finishing with each one he replaced the loop of the rod round her neck. He did this three times, each slave receiving eighteen strokes in total, and during the last circuit they began to squeal and hop from foot to foot as the rods sliced into them.

Those customers with a finely tuned ear might have noticed that the cracks of the black girl's cane sounded hollower than the others; and those experienced in administering beatings would see that her yelps and grimaces were a trifle more theatrical.

The coda to this act of the show was a birthday treat for one of the members. He was invited onto the stage, where the centurion had him give each of the white girls six strokes of their rod. When the member turned towards the black girl the centurion held him back, and asked him to repeat the six to each of the white girls as they were guilty of greater sins.

'But this time, signore, you must punish them

more rigorously.'

The member's eyes lit up as the centurion helped him off with his jacket. He laid into the girls, his forehead perspiring with effort, and was rewarded with their yelps and twisting bodies, as well as roars from the audience. At the end the white girls stood in their posts shaking with sobs, their welts plain for everyone to see.

When the curtain fell, without further punishment of Vibia, a jeer or two might normally have been expected from the floor, but her visit to the fat man's table had been noted. No one wished to offend him, and most much preferred not to be noticed by him at all.

As the band struck up once more the brothers turned back to their grappa and their conversation.

'What about Carlo?' asked the thin one, refreshing their glasses from the bottle.

'Leave him for the time being. What he did for his sister was an honourable thing. Besides, if he becomes successful as an artist we might have better uses for him than petty forging.'

They then chatted of family concerns for a few minutes.

Meanwhile a lighter drama had taken to the stage. Two leggy blondes, dressed as schoolgirls in white blouses and tartan miniskirts, had reported to the headmaster to be disciplined for kissing each other lasciviously. The girls were new to tonight's cast but the headmaster was the centurion reincarnated. His ham-like hands spanked the girls over his knee, first with their white panties up and then with them down.

Penitently the girls came down from the stage and circulated through the room, pouting and displaying reddened bottoms to any member who wished to look. If the members so chose, and many did, they could add a few more slaps.

After the schoolgirls returned to the stage they showed that they had not learned their lesson, and when the headmaster re-entered he caught them again. They had taken off their blouses and bras and were kissing and fondling each others' breasts. Naturally he had to bend them over their school desks and beat them with a long wooden ruler, while they screwed up their faces and shrieked loudly.

The elder man paid little attention to this entertainment, but his lean brother was clearly taken with one of the schoolgirls. Tonight he had to go home to his wife, but he gave orders to Bruno to make the young lady available at the weekend.

After the curtain had fallen on the school scene the brothers arrived at the last item on the evening's agenda.

'What of Bianchi?' asked the fat man. 'I heard there was a problem with the packaging.'

'It is time he retired,' replied the other. 'Drink is making him sloppy.' His voice had a cruel edge, perhaps anticipating the scenes soon to be played out on stage.

At the start of the final performance the centurion once more led in the three naked slave girls. They stood eyes down, facing the audience.

Their wrists were bound together in front of

them. The centurion ordered them to raise their arms so the audience might see their pubes unobscured by their hands. Behind each of them was their place of punishment. In the centre a rope hung down from an unseen beam above the stage. A few feet to the left of it stood a wooden whipping post. On the other side was a large, square wooden block.

As they stood submissively before the audience the centurion read out their sentences: for Vibia, twenty lashes for stealing the pear; for Gaia and Lucia, forty and fifty lashes respectively for their lesbian affair. Lucia was deemed to have begun the affair and hence had a harsher sentence. There was a murmur of approval from the audience at the severity of the punishments.

The girls dropped their arms, turned and stood at their stations with their bottoms to the audience. The centurion was in no hurry. Working at a leisurely pace he tied the hanging rope to the cord already around the black girl's wrists. At a signal from him someone above the stage mechanically drew up the rope until the girl's arms were stretched and she had to stand on tiptoe.

The centurion removed the top half of his tunic, revealing a powerful torso. Two young maidservants appeared at his side, one holding a bowl, from which he oiled all of Vibia's body. As he massaged her the girl moaned faintly in pleasure. But when he came to her buttocks the oil was slapped on and his giant hands squeezed her until she squealed. The other maidservant handed him a towel, and after he'd carefully dried his hands she offered him the bullwhip. It was a wicked instrument with a single three foot tail in thick leather. The servants withdrew and the whipping began.

All twenty strokes were delivered to Vibia's upper back. He was careful to let no lash hit her bottom, which was to be preserved for the fat man. The girl swung and hopped as the strokes fell. By the end she was left to dangle, crying quietly, while the centurion moved on to the petite white girl.

The maidservants appeared again and Gaia's body was oiled with the same leisurely attention as before. Gaia was then bound to the whipping post, her hands above her head, her feet and waist tied tightly to the post. She looked too slight to survive forty lashes, but survive them she did. Her boyish buttocks could be seen to clench as the thick tail bit into them. She struggled in vain against the cords which bound her. Her screams rent the club and her trim back and bottom soon became an angry montage of welts. The third girl cowered at her station, nervously watching, knowing worse was soon to be visited upon her.

And then her time came. Gaia's keening continued while Lucia's body was ritually oiled. She was bent over the block, her wrists and ankles tied to iron rings fitted to its front and back. Her hands were still together, fastened to the back, but her feet were apart, one tied to each side of the front of the base. Thus her sex was displayed to the audience, and as he bound her in place they could hear her frightened whispering.

The centurion faced the audience and told them that the girl had asked him to make her strokes as light as possible. He asked them what they thought he should do about it.

'Make them harder!' urged several people.

'Give her more lashes!' shouted others.

'I'll do both,' said the centurion, and turned back to the girl, who hearing her fate had begun to sob.

His first lashes bit across the girl's back, presented to him on the block. As Gaia's sobs died down, so Lucia's agonised cries replaced them. With each vicious stroke her head jerked up, before sinking back down beyond the block. The centurion proceeded to whip the backs of her thighs. Her body yanked against its restraints. He left her lovely bottom for the last, but not least, score of lashes.

By then her wails and shrieks had become a perpetual undulation, punctuated by deep gulps of breath. Her legs and buttocks were red raw. The club had never before witnessed such a spectacular whipping.

One by one the slaves were untied and led away, supported by the two maidservants. Lucia could barely walk, so the centurion hoisted her onto his back and the group left the stage.

The curtain fell and the members clapped enthusiastically until it rose five minutes later for the curtain call. Once more the naked women stood facing the audience and, on their master's command, turned to present their backs for inspection. Cowed and shivering, the white girls were weeping still. Their flayed buttocks and backs made a compelling sight for the members. Finally they put their arms on each others' shoulders and circled again as the Three Graces, before leaving the stage to ecstatic applause.

A little before his name was mentioned at the club, Bianchi stumbled out of his local watering hole. His progress along the badly lit street was far from straight, but over the years he had perfected a sine curve stagger which served him effectively enough in his cups. Ahead he could blearily make out a thin dark figure stopped at a shop window lighting a cigarette.

Bianchi crossed the road. He was a man for whom safety was ever the best policy. The easiest way to avoid trouble at night was to steer clear of men under forty. Further along the street he looked over his shoulder. The man was still looking in the window.

Suddenly the cold of the night hit Bianchi. He shivered, but decided to take a slightly longer route back; one on wider, well lit roads.

Ten minutes later he stepped from the Via Battaglia into his own small street. His tiny flat was just a few metres away. There was some sauce to heat up and some kind of dried pasta in the cupboard, he was sure. So far today he had eaten only a sandwich at lunchtime, but he wasn't hungry. It was mostly out of habit that he took in solids.

The window shopper was waiting in the shadow of his doorway, holding a silenced pistol. When Bianchi saw him he stopped. He was afraid, but it would have been pointless to run, even if he had been young and sober.

'At least,' he consoled himself, 'it isn't a painful death.'

No one in the *La Pera* audience would have begrudged the black girl her gentle treatment had they later been present in the elder brother's pied-à-terre in central Milan. Like Carlo, he too had a cathedral view, but there the similarities between the two apartments ended. This was a spacious penthouse, and although the building was old and faded, the fittings and furniture were modern and luxurious. The brothers lived for the future, not for the past. Their only interest in antiquity was the money which could be made from it.

Once again her inspection started with her luscious bottom over his lap. When his pats turned to slaps she knew her night had begun in earnest. Dressed as a maid, with apron but no skirt, high heels and stay up white stockings, the girl served him Vin Santo. He popped dark chocolates into his mouth and sipped the wine, watching her pretend to clean the room with a feather duster. When he was unhappy with her work she would be called over to touch her toes, and with the stick of the feather duster he would give her six of the best.

The fat man enjoyed this game for perhaps an hour, after which the girl was stripped naked and made to lie facedown on his splendid glass dining table. Her head rested on a pillow. Cuffs were secured round her wrists and ankles and tied to the four legs of the table. Then using a whip identical to the centurion's he lashed every inch of her body from the backs of her thighs to her shoulders. He showed no mercy in revisiting the part of her back that had already suffered in the show, and the girl sobbed into the pillow and soaked it with her tears. In between groups of lashes he used the whip's handle to toy with her anus. She had not signed up for such treatment, but she knew with this man that meek submission meant survival.

After the fat man had whipped her he led her into his bedroom. Lying on his enormous bed he grasped her hair and moved her face to the erect penis peeking up from below his large gut. He found the extra moistness of the lips and mouth of a sniffling woman an exquisite refinement to the pleasure of fellatio. Her tears, dripping into his pubic hair, were little drops of joy, and to ensure they continued he would reach out from time to time to clip her flank with a crop.

Chapter 14

Waiting, fastened to the post, Rebecca remembered the last time she had been in these stables. It had been a defining moment in her life. One weekend they had driven over to the riding school where James usually kept his horses. The idea was to ride them to his house, leave them in his stables overnight and ride them back on the Sunday.

By this time they had been dating for few weeks, but only once had he shown himself willing to discipline her. Apart from that skirmish over breast implants, which had produced such promising results, Rebecca had been treading carefully. With the relationship still in its early stages she did not want to frighten James away. Yet, when she remembered how other boyfriends had crumbled in the face of her temper, she hoped for some early reassurance that he could handle her at her most headstrong. As it turned out, she got rather more reassurance than she bargained for.

The day had started out well. Rebecca was wearing pristine white breeches, which she had bought especially for this first ride with James, and which left nothing to the imagination about her shapely curves. They were more expensive than she usually wore for everyday riding, but it was a good investment because James had barely taken his eyes off her hips and bottom until she mounted the horse.

She was an excellent rider, but she and the horse did not establish a good rapport. Perhaps Rebecca had been too concerned with James to give the young chestnut mare her proper attention. Perhaps the mare herself was disappointed not to be ridden by James. Although he rode both horses from time to time, his favourite was the chestnut, Brownie. Brownie was younger and fitter than the grey mare, so he'd offered her to Rebecca.

At first the mare was restless and frisky, but Rebecca managed to control her and they set off at a steady walk across the fields, chatting happily. After riding briskly for half an hour they had a race across an open hillside to a small copse at the top. In a closely run contest James was careful to lose. He was being polite; he was still learning about Rebecca and had not yet understood her highly competitive nature. From childhood she had resented not being taken seriously as an opponent. Because the challenges to which she responded most enthusiastically were against men, her resentment was all the greater when a man let her win.

Although it rankled with her she realised he had not meant to patronise her, so she kept her cool. They dismounted to admire the views over South Oxfordshire and Berkshire and to give the horses a rest. He flopped to the ground, but reluctant to let the damp grass stain her breeches, she leaned against a tree. She listened while he recounted some tale from local history, then when he called her over she admitted why she wouldn't sit down. So in response James stretched out his legs and invited her sit on them.

'I'll keep you off the ground,' he promised.

She lowered herself onto his lap and stretched her legs in front of her, resting them on his. James pulled her to him and kissed her neck. His erection pushed into her bottom. He ran his hands over her hips. She felt helpless in this position, but she let him caress her to his heart's content.

'Brownie is looking at us disapprovingly,' she laughed, and hearing her name the horse gave a brief blow and turned away in disdain.

He laughed too, but his caresses were becoming more amorous. She heard his breathing quicken. He kissed her ears and hair, and squeezed her breasts through the fleece she wore. His hands roamed over her hips and thighs.

'You're not wearing panties beneath your breeches, are you?' he said, faking shock, as though he'd caught her red-handed in some peccadillo.

'No,' she admitted. Rebecca had thought it best to avoid the panty-line problem today, and she never found thongs comfortable for riding.

James began to probe between her legs. 'Stop it,' she laughed.

He did so, but whispered, 'We could make love like this. You could stay on top to keep dry.'

'No, it's too open,' she said, 'and anyway it would distress the horses.'

He groaned in acquiescence. 'If only there were a cold shower handy,' he muttered.

As they were getting up James found that his left leg had gone to sleep and he stumbled against her. Rebecca was still finding her balance and fell forward onto the ground on all fours. When she rose her knees were green and wet.

'Now look what you've done!' she said angrily.

'I'm sorry.'

The sound of genuine apology in his voice placated her, until he continued, 'For a keen rider you seem very fussy about your clothes.'

Rebecca flushed hotly at this remark. She was an adventurous rider who could cope with the odd tumble and normally she didn't mind if her clothes were snagged or mud-splashed, but today she wanted to look her best for him. But being a man he was too stupid to see that.

She mounted, still in a huff, unsettling Brownie again. Resentful of his remark Rebecca decided to show James what she could do on a horse. As soon as he was up she galloped off down the hill. She could hear James' astonished cries disappearing on the wind behind her. After a few minutes he caught her up.

'What on earth's the matter?' he panted. 'This can't be about my stumble can it?'

She ignored the question, but slowed to a walk. 'Let's have a proper race, to the pond on your land,' she said, 'and this time you don't have to let me win.'

She tapped her heels firmly into Brownie, leaned forward and urged the horse into a gallop. James responded to her challenge and galloped after her. Soon he was just in the lead. Rebecca smacked the whip on her boot to stir her horse. She regained the lead but it was tight. Normally she never hit a horse but she was determined to win. She gave Brownie several sharp swats on her rump. It made little difference to poor Brownie's speed; the horse was already running as fast as she could. If anything the rough treatment caused her to slow. In the end she won by a length, but by rights it should have been more since Brownie was a faster horse than the grey.

While they rubbed down the horses in the stable yard James said nothing, but Rebecca knew he was livid, and she had to admit he had good cause.

Any host would be annoyed at a guest who mistreated his favourite animal. After they had carried the tack into the stables she was about to go out to bring Brownie into her stall, but James held her back.

'They're safely tethered,' he said. 'They can wait for a few minutes.'

He closed the stable door and picked up a thick wooden block, probably used to wedge it open sometimes. Rebecca sensed the gathering storm and decided to take the offensive. She complained vehemently about his condescending manner. When he said nothing but led her to the end of the stalls she pretended to be outraged by the lecherous way he had held her on the hillside. All in all she must have lambasted him for five minutes, during which time James said nothing. Eventually she shouted herself silent.

He lay the block flush with the outside wall of the end stall. She could read his thoughts: if she stood on the block the top of the wall would be waist high and she could bend over it.

'You can't just spank me whenever you feel like it!' she snapped.

'I'll spank you when you deserve it,' he replied grimly.

'You're always spanking me!' she protested. In fact, apart from that first slap on the rear at the restaurant he had only spanked her once.

'If you kept your temper in check I wouldn't need to.'

She tried to run for the door but he moved surprisingly quickly, caught her round the waist and wedged her against his side. He had a very strong grip. There was a moment when both of them were motionless, breathing deeply. Then he laid into her backside with his hand. She struggled, but not very convincingly as without pausing the spanking he manoeuvred her to the wall so she could support herself against it. After that she didn't bother to struggle at all. Nor did she cry out. She just grimaced into the wall and absorbed the stinging slaps. He stopped and cupped his hand over her now flaming buttocks. The new material of her breeches was getting some early extra wear. When he started to speak she anticipated him and slid her breeches down without being asked.

'God you have a beautiful behind,' he said in appreciation, and ran his hand around it.

'"Callipygian", someone once called it,' she said, just for the sake of a reply.

That made him chuckle, but when the spanks resumed they were no more gentle. By the time he decided she'd been punished enough her face was screwed up with pain. It had been even harder than his first effort in the drawing room. Nor was it over, it seemed.

As he released her she started to pull up her breeches, but he stayed her hand. 'Not yet,' he said. 'I think today's outburst deserves a special reward.'

He went to the tack store and returned with a riding crop.

'You must be joking!' she gasped.

'You were ready enough to use it on poor

Brownie. I counted seven swats, so that's how many you'll have.'

He took her by the hand and led her back to the end wall of the stall. With her pants around her knees she stumbled along, holding them up with her free hand.

When they arrived at the block he told her to take off her boots and breeches. She could leave on her top and fleece. She mounted the block. She had to stretch on tiptoe to be able to bend over the stall.

Rebecca's expectation that he would flick her with the tongue of the crop was rudely shattered by the first piercing crack. The tongue had indeed hit her right cheek, but it was the shaft of the crop which cut across her left. She got off the block and danced around in front of him, gripping her buttocks in her hands and yelling profanities at him. Later in their relationship she would get several extra strokes for such a performance, but today he took pity on her, in her first true beating.

Rebecca recovered her poise and decided to show him that she was not completely cowed. Once she resumed her tiptoe stance on the block she said, 'One, Sir James,' in a slightly mocking tone.

Mocking your torturer is probably not a wise policy, she thought, and the next six strokes were to prove she was right. Outside she could hear the horses snorting restlessly at her howls, but she took her punishment well and counted the strokes, although unasked.

He held her in his arms while the pain subsided,

stroking her hair, and she was thrilled when he told her how much he admired her bravery.

'You handled yourself like a lady,' he said seriously, and she smiled at the outdated phrase, which nonetheless was welcome to her ears. James believed that how people coped with adversity was a good guide to their true character. He kissed her upturned face.

Then he dropped his trousers and fucked her. To get better purchase he put his forearm under her bottom and drew her onto him, her yelps of pain at this new assault on her aching bum ignored.

Afterwards she dressed and went out to fetch the horses, and needless to say the stall over which she had been beaten belonged to Brownie.

Examining herself in the mirror later, she found that while the whole of her bottom was red and bruised, seven neat parallel stripes of the crop showed on her left buttock alone. It was plain that James knew well how to wield a crop. At the time she remembered wondering what other weapons were in his armoury, and of course, by now she had found out.

On Sunday her bottom was still so sore that she couldn't ride and James had to call the stables to collect the horses. They spent a peaceful day together, free from emotional storms. Rebecca had her reassurance and James had her heart.

Her thoughts returned to the present. Another landmark of her life was now to be played out in the same stables.

She fretted over whether this was the best set up. Her footwear had been discussed at length with Nicola. It was far too cold for her to be barefoot. Nicola had proposed high heels, but Rebecca did not think them appropriate to the stables. Instead she had chosen her riding boots and polished them well. Even without her breeches the soft brown leather fitted snugly to her calves.

They had mulled over, too, whether or not Rebecca's feet should be tied to the post. In the end they decided not, thinking he might prefer to see her dance with the sting of the whip.

Apart from the boots her only adornment was the diamond choker around her neck. She knew it was rude to wear it before James had formally given it to her, but it sent a clear message that she was ready to be his once more. And if he was that bothered about the poor etiquette he could whip her for that too; it would be fine by her.

The sound of feet crunching in the snow-covered yard brought her out of her reverie. She hoped it was James, or else she was going to be very embarrassed indeed. There was someone at the stable door. She sensed it was him, hearing his exclamation as he entered. She said nothing, staring meekly at the post, but when he called her name in a way which showed his happiness at seeing her, she turned to him with tears in her eyes.

Early on Sunday morning James brooded in his study. Their flight was in a few hours. Having slept on his decision time was running out to call the police.

Hearing a knock at the front door he went to the window. It was a freezing, sunny day. A thick covering of snow had fallen in the night, making a perfect winter landscape.

He was enormously relieved to see Nicola; all the more so because Carlo was not with her. When he opened the door she stood on the step, smiling up at him. She wore a woolly hat and a thick sheepskin coat over her jeans and furry boots. The tip of her nose was red from the cold. She looked utterly delightful and he felt a pang of regret that she would no longer be gracing his study, let alone his lap.

She refused his invitation to come into the house, even though she was shivering.

'Where is your car?' he asked, puzzled. The snow on the drive was unbroken by tyre tracks.

'I came in at the back gate and parked near the stables,' she explained. 'Hope that's okay.'

'Yes, of course.'

'I've only just played my messages,' she said sheepishly. 'We were out last night.'

'I left it yesterday morning,' he replied irritably.

'Sorry, yes. Carlo and I were a bit, um...' she hesitated, '...preoccupied most of the day. To be honest, I'd hoped you wouldn't realise they were gone.'

'Why did you take them?' he asked, perplexed.

'I only borrowed them, James,' she said soothingly. 'You said I'm like a daughter to you now. I wouldn't steal from you.'

'I know, Nick,' he sighed. 'But what did you want them for?'

Instead of replying she handed him the small blue box containing the engagement ring. He put it in his pocket, expecting the larger box with the choker to follow. 'Where's the necklace?' he asked.

'In the stables.'

'What do you mean?' He was losing patience with her bizarre behaviour. 'What's it doing there of all places?'

Nicola hugged him to calm him down, and instinctively James hugged her back.

'The necklace isn't important,' she said. 'There's something else in the stables, too.'

'Not important?' He made to break away, but she clung to him harder and kissed him on the cheek.

'Don't be dumb, James,' she whispered in his ear. 'You can put two and two together, can't you?'

He stared at her in bewilderment as she stepped back onto the drive. He had the uneasy feeling that their roles had been reversed, and she was now instructing him. But what the subject was he wasn't sure.

'Got to go,' she said brightly. 'We're leaving for the airport soon.'

She blew him a kiss and padded off round the back of the house. James called for her to wait, then ran back to grab a coat before trudging after her. By the time he got there Nicola was driving through the gates.

James cursed and plodded along to the stables. If she thought he knew what she was up to she was crediting him with more intelligence than he had. As he approached the stable door he was met by a wall of warm air. Someone, presumably Nicola, had turned the stables heating on high.

Propped just inside the open door was the finished portrait of Rebecca in white. Here was the 'something else' Nicola had mentioned. The face in the painting was very lovely and rather sad. Gazing back at her he too felt inconsolably sad.

A rustle to his left startled him, and when he turned to see what it was he was more startled still. Rebecca stood facing a wooden post in the wall. Her arms were held high above her head. Her wrists were bound by leather handcuffs which had been looped over a hook in the post. She was naked apart from riding boots.

'Rebecca!'

When she heard his voice she turned to him. He went up to her and held his body against hers. Her chestnut hair fell down her back. He nestled his face in it and kissed her shoulder. Around her neck was the diamond choker.

'Thank you for the necklace,' she said. 'It's a wonderful present.'

'Nicola was right,' he whispered, 'it's not important compared to having you back.'

'Don't be angry with her for taking it.'

'I'm not. She was only making sure it went to its rightful home.'

'Have you the ring?' she asked.

He remembered it was in his pocket and he reached up and slipped it on her finger.

'Now you need to finish off what Carlo started,' she told him. 'Really, it was your job all along, but you were not to know what I'd done to Nicola.'

On a ledge in the wall lay the flogger James had seen Carlo using on Christmas Eve. He picked it up. Once again, he thought, I have the whip hand, but they seem to have been in control. He could live with that, he thought, if it meant regaining Rebecca.

'How many?' he asked, taking off his coat and rolling up his sleeves.

'That's for you to decide,' she replied.

He gently swept her hair over her shoulder, leaving her back bare.

'Nicola told me that Carlo gave her forty lashes.'

She nodded.

'So you shall have fifty,' he declared, watching her closely.

She smiled wanly at him. 'You know me so well,' she said.

The whipping had been terrible, of course, but at least Carlo's truncated effort had taught her what to expect. She danced and swung on the hook, sometimes screaming obscenities through gritted teeth. The more extreme of these earned extras, but James was lenient in view of the overall severity of the flogging. Rebecca didn't faint; she felt every excruciating lash, but with each had also come the joy of knowing she had James back.

Afterwards he lifted her down and draped his coat around her shoulders. He offered to carry her in his arms, but her bottom and back was too painful.

She tried to stagger along supported by his arm,

and when her legs gave way he stooped, held her around the knees and hoisted her over his shoulder in a fireman's lift.

'Time for me to carry you off like a caveman,' he said as he picked her up.

A spark of her old fire returned. 'Except your cave has eight beds and five reception rooms,' she quipped quietly into his back.

He took her to his bedroom and fetched a hot drink. After tenderly treating her wounds he left her to rest for a couple of hours.

She lay on his bed, beaten but triumphant. James knew her better than anyone, she thought, except perhaps her mother. Her insatiable competitive streak, her hot-headed tendency to go too far, and her innate sense of justice, which required that her excesses were punished. From the outset his refusal to accept Rebecca's wilful behaviour had satisfied a profound need within her. He had a natural authority she could submit to, and it made her life at once richer and more ordered in consequence.

The change in her was noticed at work; her latest promotion had come as a consequence of a widely perceived improvement in her self-control. There was even talk of a directorship in the not too distant future.

After a while Rebecca drifted off to sleep. She and Nicola had been up late the night before planning what to do. Once again Carlo had been banished to the village pub.

When she awoke James was there with a tray and some food. He sat beside her on the bed. They ate chicken soup and beef sandwiches and drank some burgundy. Afterwards they made love. She sat astride him, trying as best she could to avoid pressing her injuries.

For the rest of the day they lay on the bed talking contentedly. They speculated as to whether the relationship between Nicola and Carlo would last. James was inclined to think not.

'Do you think the police will find out that Carlo was the forger?' she asked.

'They already know he was.'

'What?' Rebecca pushed herself up from the bed, ignoring the stab of pain it caused.

'Don't worry,' he soothed her, 'your contract with Carlo is safe. Even if they could build a watertight case against him it was hardly the crime of the century. The forgeries weren't even sold.'

He went on to describe his meeting at Scotland Yard on Christmas Eve. Officers from the Milanese Questura had been present, and they were after much fatter fish than Carlo. Pursuing him would cause a commotion that wouldn't be helpful to their wider investigation.

'They also told me why he needed the money.'

James related Maria's tragic story. Rebecca was silent for a time. She remembered Carlo's worried frown that night at the bar in Milan after he had phoned his sister. It seemed so long ago. The mention of Christmas Eve reminded her too of the nadir of her life.

'So he isn't a total shit after all,' she said. She was pleased for Nicola's sake, but for her own she would have preferred to be able to hate him unreservedly for what he did to her that afternoon, and how close it had come to breaking her engagement for good.

'I love you, James.'

'You're not marrying me for my eight bedroom cave, then?' he joked, kissing her.

'No, I'm not. And in the marriage ceremony I'll use the old words. I'll promise to obey you, and I'll mean it.'

Truthfulness and faithfulness would be cornerstones of their marriage, they agreed solemnly. That way, any repetition of the temptations and misunderstandings of December would be avoided. That and the fact that, from now on, Rebecca would be choosing James' secretaries.

Carlo and Nicola had splashed out on business class tickets for the flight to Milan, which had also enabled them to wait in the comfortable surroundings of the British Airways Club lounge at Heathrow. Still sore, she preferred to sit on deep cushions and avoid the jostle of crowds. Forgetting to remove a cheap anklet she had triggered the airport metal scanner. The female security guard frisked her and Nicola jumped in pain when she caught a sensitive spot on her hips. The guard had cast Carlo a deeply suspicious look.

He had been suitably contrite since his fall from grace on Christmas Eve. Nicola had more or less forgiven him. In his favour he had been uncharacteristically understanding about her need to fulfil the agreement with James. Would he be as sympathetic when he had her to himself in Milan, she wondered?

Certainly he had hated her doing it. When he had returned to the flat on Saturday morning he scrutinised her stripes and bruises carefully, mortified to find they were worse than he'd inflicted at the cottage.

'It's not a competition, Carlo,' she had chided him, yet she wondered if, in a way, for him it was. If so, James had won by a whisker, and she meant it to be a long time before Carlo could try to outdo him. The degree and frequency of her punishments in recent weeks had turned a sublime joy into a trial by fire. For the coming few months her misdemeanours would be of the merely spankable variety.

After inspecting her damaged skin Carlo had first worked his wonders with the lotion, and then his wonders with her body. Whatever Carlo's skills as a painter there was one art form in which he was a consummate master.

After the small airline meal he held her hand and talked to her about his hopes for the future. His commissions included some commercial art work for an advertising company, which was lucrative business. Together with the contract for Rebecca's firm and the removal of the shadow of his debt to the syndicate, it meant he was feeling more secure financially. He thought they might look for a larger flat, because his studio was really too small for two people.

Nicola let him talk. She liked the fact that his

plans reflected her needs as well. The idea of moving to a new place, which she could help choose and decorate, was appealing. According to Rebecca his bachelor pad was a bit grim.

She considered how her one little disobedience with James' shares had brought her so much suffering, and so much joy. She had won through trying times, and a more mature and confident young woman had emerged. Who knew what she was capable of if she put her mind to it?

At least there was the glimmer of a job for her. A friend of Carlo's had told him that a language professor at Milan University needed a secretarial assistant, and for reasons which were not entirely clear the professor preferred English applicants.

Maybe life with Carlo would work out well, but she wasn't building her hopes up yet; there were too many imponderables.

That story about his sister was very strange. She wasn't sure she believed it; it sounded like something from an old gangster film. Could an innocent girl in modern Italy be caught so easily in the web of organised crime? Perhaps he had embellished it to put himself in a good light after screwing up so badly with Rebecca.

The thought of Rebecca reminded her of the morning's stratagem in the stables. She prayed it had worked well. Rebecca had promised to call her later to let her know, and it would be good to get a call from England on her first night away. She would warn her that James was to feel free to use his new piece of furniture. Somehow, she thought, if Rebecca were to share the bonds that had once held her, it would cement their newfound friendship.

Maria drank coffee in Linate airport, awaiting her flight to London. She frowned with disapproval at some young Englishmen lounging untidily across more seats than they needed. Eleven in the morning and they were already drinking beer heavily. They were dressed in combat trousers, as though about to undertake guerrilla warfare rather than board a civilian flight. Maria hoped they were not representative of men in London.

Yet they could not dim the thrill she felt at escaping Italy to begin afresh. A *strada senza uscita* had miraculously opened up into a piazza of possibilities.

La Pera had given her an excellent reference which had landed her a job as a waitress in an Italian restaurant. It seemed sensible to ease herself into her new life in London in an environment where her Italian upbringing would help. She hoped against hope that the place had no mob connections. If she suspected any she would leave at once.

Carlo had told her that London was an expensive city, but Maria knew it was also vibrant and full of opportunities. She had a few thousand in savings as a cushion. Although her line of work had rarely been pleasurable, it had been well paid. The girls were allowed to keep nearly all their tips, because the managers knew they would try harder to please the customers that way. Maria supposed she had been fortunate in ending up in places catering for the discerning wealthy, but her natural beauty had helped her. There were other houses where the girls became drug addicted fodder to be discarded once they were no longer able to function. Drugs had not been pressed on her, and although she'd experimented a little she had never come close to addiction.

Nearing twenty, Maria felt much wiser than she was when she'd become infatuated with the well dressed hunks in her home town of Catanzaro in the south. Their expensive clothes, flash cars and full wallets, the deference they were shown in the streets, their superficial good looks had lured her into what seemed an exciting world. Only later did she realise it was squalid, brutal and empty. After a short stint as girlfriend to a minor henchman she was packed off to Milan, far away from friends and family.

Although well treated and not exactly a prisoner, it was made clear to her that attempts to escape would be dealt with mercilessly. Two of the girls with whom she worked were made an example of, and were no longer beautiful in consequence. Passports were taken from them so they could not stray too far. In any case, for Maria a life on the run and in fear would have been no life. Going to the police was pointless. Even if you found someone who wasn't corrupt, your family was still vulnerable. Too ashamed to phone her mother she had retreated into an alien existence.

Carlo was her hero. After their mother died he tracked her down in Milan and bought her life back for her. There had been some last minute hitch with the money, but he came through for her. It seemed he had a new English girlfriend, and Maria hoped they would meet soon. It was a pity they had missed each other, crossing between Italy and England.

She wondered whether the English girl knew about Carlo's sexual preferences. Probably she did. Maria had known since she was thirteen. From the top of the stairs one night she'd peeped down, goggle-eyed, as her eighteen year old brother bent her babysitter over the kitchen table and spanked her with a wooden spoon. It seemed Carlo had just come home and caught her smoking his cigarettes. And thereafter Maria's mother had been bemused by how often and how eagerly the girl volunteered to babysit for her. Unluckily for the girl she was never to see Carlo again; he was rarely home before their mother and soon afterwards he went off to college.

Her thoughts took Maria back to the night Filippo had spanked and strapped her. He hadn't hurt her at all really, just wounded her pride. He had promised to spend a weekend in London once she was settled. When he did Maria intended to be a little bit naughty, and to let Filippo decide what he ought to do about it.